THE MIRROR

US ARMY SFC (RET), WILLIAM A. STEPHENS JR.

The views presented are those of the author and do not necessarily represent the official policy or position of the Department of the Army, Department of Defense, or the US government.

BookVenture Publishing LLC
1000 Country Lane Ste 300
Ishpeming MI 49849
www.bookventure.com
Hotline: 1(877) 276-9751
Fax: 1(877) 864-1686

Ordering Information:
Quantity sales. Special discounts are available on quantity purchases by corporations, associations, and others. For details, contact the publisher at the address above.

Printed in the United States of America.

Library of Congress Control Number		APPLIED
ISBN-13:	Softcover	978-1-64166-323-6
	Hardcover	978-1-64348-878-3
	Pdf	978-1-64166-324-3
	ePub	978-1-64166-325-0
	Kindle	978-1-64166-326-7

Rev. date: 12/08/2017

CONTENTS

FOREWORD

The title of this book of poems, *The Mirror*, not only defines the content of the contemporary and lifelong generated poems of William "Bill" A. Stephens Jr., but it is also explanatory of poetry in general. The composition of a poem is the manifestation of feelings and thoughts and words onto paper by an individual that has served his country proudly. It is the conveyance of ordinary words into other more poetic words while the reader is confronted with the task to reestablish the origin of metaphoric words that relate to an individual that is dealing with Post-Traumatic Stress Disorder (PTSD).

The meaning behind the title of this poetry lies in the fact that Stephens mainly works on poetry that is a reflection of what he actually sees when he looks into the mirror and therefore suggests various levels of perception, interpretation, and the consequent formulation of meaning when soldiers return from the battlefield. Stephens uses metaphoric references, evocative phrases, and word play to evoke virtual feelings those that are often held inside our warriors for months and sometimes years following their return back to what we would normally think of as a "normal life." Here is a great example of what you will experience:

Bullet to the Brain

You're standing in a room with a candle burning bright.
In one hand, you're holding a revolver with bullet in the chamber.
You're playing the game.
One shot, one kill.

US Army SFC (Ret), William A. Stephens Jr.

Poetry written and published by Bill Stephens is dynamic, immediate, and powerful. Mainly focusing on patriotic, nature, and love poems, he endeavors to be honest with a hint of humor—clear about the dilemma of the tension between reality and dream, within a spiritual and predestined awareness of those symptoms experienced by warriors on the battlefield that have left so many confused and untrusting.

> *In the other you're holding a rose.*
> *The petals are falling one by one.*
> *She loves me, she me loves not.*
> *This is the love game.*

> *So!*

Yet once again hope surfaces in the following:

> *What's your choice?*
> *the bullet to the brain*
> *Or*
> *The women who drove you insane.*

Words published in a book share one connecting principle: the writer must touch the reader with these words—the eyes become the vision of the poem, the actual touch of feeling. But, as is the case with all visions, Stephens reaches the conclusion:

> *Living on the Razor's Edge*

> *Playing with life because you have nothing left. You go faster and faster that you don't want to stop. The only thing that will stop you is the object that you hit next. Always taking a chance because nothing ever happens to you. Just waiting for death and time to both meet you in the right place, and then you rest and play these little games no more.*

Although Stephens' work portrays the conflict between his inner self and the battlefield on the one hand, it also confronts the lack of trust that many soldiers who suffer from PTSD and other disabilities must face upon their return back to reality and the reintegration back into day-to-day life for many of our warriors in society today. There are many complexities of PTSD, and those feelings that are experienced by each individual, with no one experience being the same.

Who is Stephens? Sergeant First Class William "Bill" A. Stephens Jr. (Ret.) was born in Carlisle, Pennsylvania, in 1969. Upon graduating from Carlisle Senior High School, Mr. Stephens enlisted in the United States Army in October 1988. Throughout his twenty years of distinguished military service, he has held positions of leadership ranging in experience from Cannoneer, Senior Enlisted Advisor, Battalion Career Counselor, Battalion Intelligence Sergeant, Senior Observer Controller Trainer, and Battalion Security Manager. Upon retirement from the military with distinction, Mr. Stephens continued leadership roles in the civilian workforce through completion of an internship with the Defense Security Service, a Pennsylvania State Corrections Officer, a Department of the Defense Employee.

Mr. Stephens' assignments include Mechanicsburg, Camp Hill, New Cumberland, Pennsylvania. His military assignments include Fort Dix, New Jersey; Fort Sill, Oklahoma; Fort Lewis, Washington; Fort Carson, Colorado; Fort Riley, Kansas and Walter Reed Army Medical Center, Washington, D. C., as a part of the Wounded Warrior Transition Brigade. Mr. Stephens deployed multiple times to overseas locations including four combat deployments to Kuwait/Saudi Arabia as a part of *Operation Desert Shield* and *Operation Desert Storm*. In 2006, he completed four tours to Iraq and Southwest Asia as a part of *Operation Iraqi Freedom/Liberation of Iraq*, the *Transition of Iraq*, and *National Resolution of Iraq* where his assignment was instrumental in collecting battlefield strategy data. As a result of his research efforts and compilation of "war" data, Mr. Stephens developed the Security Forces Handbook as a significant contributing author for the *Center of Army Lessons Learned*. This handbook was mandated for soldiers deploying to battlefield locations to provide better insight and real-life examples for soldiers as well as to limit casualties in the war zones.

He is a graduate of the Army's First Sergeant Course where he was selected as the First Sergeant of his class and has completed all levels of leadership courses throughout the Army. He is a graduate of the Army Antiterrorism Level I and Level II Course, Security Managers Course, and Total Army Instructor Trainers Course. Just before graduation from college with a degree in Leadership, he turned his focus toward Personnel Security. Upon retirement, Mr. Stephens graduated as the Student Leader of his class in 2009 from the Class 667C Pennsylvania Department of Corrections Training Academy. He is working on the Physical Security Course and the Department of Defense Security Professional Education Development Program.

Military awards received include the Joint Service Commendation Medal, (3) Meritorious Service Medals, (10) Army Commendation Medals, (10) Army Achievement Medals, Military Outstanding Volunteer Service Medal, Southwest Asia Service Medal with (3) Bronze Campaign Stars, and the Iraq Campaign Medal with (3) Bronze Service Stars. Mr. Stephens was recognized for his efforts by receipt of the "Major General Aubrey Red Newman award for Outstanding Leadership" as well as being a member of the Sergeant Audie Murphy Club. He is an active member of the Wounded Warrior Project and provides presentations to other veterans on behalf of the project. In 2011–12, Mr. Stephens was recognized for his hard work by the Combined Federal Campaign (CFC) and received the Central Pennsylvania Golden Star Leaders Award. In his spare time, Mr. Stephens volunteers as a CFC Campaign coordinator, assists with the Navy's Pennsylvania Adult Special Olympics, and the installation's children's Christmas Program for disadvantaged youth.

Stephens has written poetry from the countryside of Bavaria, Nuremberg, Germany, to the sands of South West Asia (Iraq/Kuwait/Saudi Arabia), and the rice paddies of South Korea. He has written poetry from Mt. Rainier, Fort Lewis, Washington, to Pikes Peak, Fort Carson, Colorado, to the home of the Field Artillery, Fort Sill, Oklahoma, and the "Land of Oz," Fort Riley, Kansas. He was inspired during deployment after deployment and combat operation after combat operation, when he didn't have treatment, when he spent long nights in the field in Kuwait and during the times he feared he would never return home. Stephens wrote these poems as a coping mechanism; his book and poems can help struggling veterans with mental disorders and help their families as well. There is no place like home Carlisle, Pennsylvania.

The poems suggest a psychological condition of control, and Stephen's norms and values are tested in a unique compilation of words and thoughts during some of the toughest times in his life. His use of a dream-reality becomes possible—words are crucial to the evocation of the untouchable depression our warriors experience during the long nights in the trenches. The eyes replace all other senses of the readers within the contents of this book. Sight provides the link between the depression, anxiety, the word, the soul, and the link to Bill Stephen's poems. Enjoy.

Colonel Mikel Burroughs (Ret.), US Army
Castle Rock, Colorado

PREFACE

PTSD—four simple letters—Post-Traumatic Stress Disorder, the wound that you cannot see. Simply defined by the Mayo Clinic as "'a mental health condition that's triggered by a terrifying event—either experiencing it or witnessing it. Symptoms may include flashbacks, nightmares, and severe anxiety, as well as uncontrollable thoughts about the event."

Very neatly explained. Sounds simple and easy to treat, right? *Wrong!*

What PTSD really means is, "I have stood at the gates of hell and looked inside. That horrible memory is with me constantly, and I will carry it with me forever."

Probably the worst part of PTSD is that no one can really understand or relate to the veteran other than his brothers-in-arms who have had similar experiences. Family members do not have the ability to fully understand what the sufferer is going through, and many times their response is to "'get over it'" or "'snap out of it'" or worse. They don't understand the intensity of the flashbacks or how an innocent sound or aroma can trigger a terrifying response in the veteran. Nightmares and sweat-soaked bedclothes become an annoyance to the family. Violent outbreaks from the veteran can scare the family. Episodes of depression or mood swings are not understood by the family. All these things tend to distance the family from the veteran at exactly the time he or she needs love and understanding.

Perhaps this is why the therapy dogs are so valuable to so many veterans. Dogs offer unconditional love and are able to discern the mental status of their owners. They are not judgmental, and they offer infinite forgiveness and companionship. They listen without taking sides.

The VA system is often overloaded, and the response to the veteran is a prescription and an appointment for a visit in three months. The veteran is left to his own devices to cope with his symptoms.

PTSD is not new, but the recognition of this disorder is relatively new. While it can exist in civilians who have traumatic experiences, it is best known in veterans who have had prolonged intense emotional episodes, most classically related to combat. It was first officially recognized in 1980 by the American Psychiatric Association, for the first time recognizing the reason so many Vietnam veterans had these strange symptoms. Dr. Matthew Friedman notes that Shakespeare's Henry IV may have had classic PTSD.

In the Civil War, it was called soldier's heart. In World War I, it was shell shock. In World War II, it was battle fatigue. In Vietnam, it was completely ignored until 1980. In all the recent wars in the Middle East, it has properly been called PTSD.

My own uncle was in combat throughout Europe in World War II and returned as a different man to his family. No one could understand the change in Uncle George when he came home, and he suffered alone from the devil of undiagnosed PTSD, self-treating with alcohol, and he carried the twin devils of PTSD and alcoholism until his traumatic death in 1962, seventeen years after the war ended.

Some veterans find solace in writing stories or poetry about their experiences. Some paint or seek other creative outlets. Some seek out their fellow sufferers and share experiences in group therapy. Sadly, some find relief in the bottom of a bottle or at the sharp end of a needle. For some, the only relief is that of eternal rest, often at their own hand.

Since the draft is long gone, too few of our citizens have served in the Armed Forces of our country. Too few of our citizens have made sacrifices to preserve our freedom. Too *many* of our citizens cannot comprehend what our military members undergo on a daily basis to keep us safe and free.

As a nation, we ask far too much of our young men and women in uniform and we pay them far too little for what they do. They suffer multiple deployments away from family and friends, and they are exposed daily to extreme physical and mental stress. Those who have not served tend to take their freedom for granted and tend to forget what we owe to our troops.

Billy's book will reveal the personal journey with PTSD of just one of our many troops who suffer from that disorder. Billy served his country honorably and well in the United States Army where he defended our freedom at the sacrifice of his own family life. Billy will continue to fight this burden for a long time, and hopefully, with the help of God and his fellow Americans, he will finally find the ability to cope with this devil and close those gates of hell forever.

Best of luck, Billy, and God bless you.
Thank you for your service and your sacrifice, my brother.

Dr. Robert F. Hall
LCDR, MC
US Navy (Ret.)
Carlisle, Pennsylvania

INTRODUCTION

This book is about short stories and poems. It dates back to my early deployments in Desert Shield and Desert Storm and continues to the present day as I sit down to write night after night. At one time I used to laugh and joke around, but after I saw my life pass right in front of my eyes, I lost my funny bone. Throughout these trying years, I have needed to express my thoughts and pain to others. To some I just appeared to be stressed. No one wanted to listen to what I needed to say.

The time has come to release all the darkness that I've been hiding from everyone and to share my experiences with you. As a small boy I always wanted to be a soldier at war, and I grew into a man that has seen the darkness and fear of a combat zone. For years and years, I've been hiding behind this curtain. You first have to understand my words of wisdom before you can understand me. What you are about to read on the next few pages might therapeutically help you understand what I'm trying to say to you.

Just like a beginning, there is an end. Soon you will have many questions flowing through your minds. For many years, everything to me has been a mystery until now.

As an author, I tried to express different versions of Post-Traumatic Stress Disorder (PTSD) because PTSD is not just a combat disorder that I discovered through my therapy, talking to other veterans with PTSD, or just everyday people on social media sites. It is a hidden killer that we all must come together and help one another from suffering with this terrible disorder/disease.

US Army SFC (Ret), William A. Stephens Jr.

Enjoy this book of darkness, sadness, and pain that conveys all I have been put through. This book is dedicated to the nonbeliever who told me years ago that I was nothing, would never be anything in life, and would never be a successful person. To my close friends who stuck with me and believed in me, there will always be a place in my heart for you, and I hope to see you on the other side. Someday all will know the truth, but for now I hold the key to my success.

SAM007

A ten-year-old girl sits on the couch and wonders to herself why her mommy and daddy just will never get along and why the family is not happy like all her other friends' families. As she grows up she begins to figure out that her father has a problem that she has noticed ever since she has been in her mother's womb. I noticed when I'm around, she drew pictures of her family without her daddy in them. They are posted on the refrigerator, and sometimes she doesn't even know I'm there anymore. "Why is my daddy not here, where is he, and why do mommy and daddy fight all the time?"

Post-Traumatic Stress Disorder is not just a killer inside the mind but a family killer as well. Since I came back from the battlefield, I haven't known my family as I thought I once knew them. I am now a different person but always a warrior and hero in my daughter's eyes. I hope she feels the same way I feel when she closes her eyes at night when her mommy lies beside her without a daddy to say "Good night."

SAM007

REMEMBERING THE MENTORS

The *Merriam-Webster Online Dictionary* defines a *mentor* as "a trusted counselor or guide." Others expand on that definition by suggesting that a mentor is "someone who is helping you with your career, specific work projects or general life advice out of the goodness of his or her heart."

A mentor in my own definition is one who is a guide sometime in life, someone who added a notch to the belt. A mentor is a person who stands by you and leads you down the path of *leadership*. He/She is a person who corrects your errors and makes an easier way around things. A mentor can make a hard process a simple one. They are people who help build the mold for a never-ending life and are counselors of grammar and literature having a positive influence on you.

History and Definition

The original mentor is a character in Homer's epic poem "The Odyssey." When Odysseus, king of Ithaca went to fight in the Trojan War, he entrusted the care of his kingdom to Mentor. Mentor served as the teacher and overseer of Odysseus' son, Telemachus.

We acquired "mentor" from the literature of ancient Greece. In Homer's epic "The Odyssey," Odysseus was away from home fighting and journeying for twenty years. During that time, Telemachus, the son he left as a babe in arms grew up under the supervision of Mentor, an old and trusted friend. When the goddess Athena decided it was time to complete the education of young Telemachus, she visited him disguised as Mentor and they set out together to learn about his father. Today, we use the word *mentor* for anyone who is a positive guiding influence in another (usually younger) person's life.

A mentor is a personal advocate for you, not so much in the public setting, but rather in your life. Many organizations recognize the power of effective mentoring and have established programs to help younger professionals identify and gain support from more experienced professionals in this format.

These are the last names of people who have been a positive influence or a mentor to me:

> J. Diamond, Mom and Dad, Harrison, Benitez, Mendoza, Ortiz, Bailey, Michaels, Hurt, Canudas, Magnus, Gloriod, Perez, Jackson, Moore, Chess, Tilley, Gomez, Tutu, Fregso, Dr. Hall, Coleman, Wilson, Mayor Timothy Scott, Heidecker, Rainey, Fenstermacher, Telles, Morrison, Murphy-Sweet, Miller, Steinour, Melanfant, Morrison, Michaels, Szymczak, Williams, Drill Sergeant Nicewonger, Drill Sergeant Johnson, the Staff NCO's and Officer's at the Warrior Transitions Unit (WTU), and Dr. Barber and VA Hospital.

Special thanks to the *Sentinel* newspaper and Michael Bupp of Carlisle, Pennsylvania at [mailto: MBupp@cumberlink.com] for a super cover to this book. Without you, this would not be possible.

I'd like to thank Ms. Szymczak for the first official edit of this entire book, for taking the time from her job and her family and doing this outstanding job. From the kindness of her heart, she used her knowledge and technical skills for our American veterans and surviving people who are dealing with the everyday demons of this killer disease we call Post-Traumatic Stress Disorder.

What a mentor did for my life was to change just a little something, like inspire me to write poetry, create a job resume, set me up for a job interview, made sure my dress blues were ready for the Sergeant Audie Murphy Board, or ensured the battle plan was set in stone to attack at a particular time. You covered my back when our classes were out of order during training up at Fort Dix, New Jersey. You trained me to the standard on how to be a professional civilian employee for the Department of Defense. You corrected that small grammar mistake on a soldier's counseling before the soldier saw it. You put me in my place because I was too chalky of a Noncommissioned Officer during a field exercise (Old School Training), and you stood by me as battle buddy when I needed that extra push in basic training to graduate. You were my first Howitzer Section Chief, showing me skill level 1 through 5 basic Field Artillery cannon crew member drills. You were that hard Corporal, who showed me how to be a basic soldier, and my first real Army friend. You were my battery Commander who selected me to be your driver and put up with my non-communicating radio skills. You were my first real girlfriend, someone who showed me what love was, how it felt to be wanted, and how a woman should be treated. As a mentor, you knew senior level executives in the Department of Defense and made me realize that someone always had my back. It is great to have people in the big house, if you know what I mean. I could go on forever, but there are more stories to write about and people to see.

We must remember the warriors who are suffering from PTSD. We need a mentor in our life that will guide and help us with little things around the house or just in life. Don't ever forget the ones who helped you because they are the first people that come to mind when you start thinking of mentors in your life. There are too many veterans being turned away from VA clinics with hidden signs of Desert Storm syndrome or just mild cases of PTSD that turned into traumatic cases of PTSD. Please get out and find a mentor who can help you get the help that you need!

LINKS: http://maketheconnection.net/what-is-mtc
       http://www.ptsd.va.gov/public/where-to-get-help.asp
       http://www.realwarriors.net/veterans/treatment/ptsdtreatment.php

PHONE numbers: 1-800-273-8255 PTSD HOTLINE
    Helpline: http://ptsdhotline.com

THE NEVER-ENDING
BATTLE OF PTSD
ON THE BATTLEFIELD AND BEYOND

You want to be vigilant; you want to react to strange noises; you want to sleep lightly and wake easily; you want to have flashbacks that remind you of the danger; and you want to be, by turns, anxious and depressed. Anxiety keeps you ready to fight, and depression keeps you from being too active and putting yourself at greater risk.

This is a universal human adaptation to danger that is common to other mammals as well. It may be unpleasant, but it's preferable to getting eaten. (Because Post-Traumatic Stress Disorder is so adaptive, many have begun leaving the word *disorder* out of the term to avoid stigmatizing a basically healthy reaction).

Because PTSD is a natural response to danger, it's almost unavoidable in the short-term and mostly self-correcting in the long-term. Only about 20 percent of people exposed to trauma react with long-term (chronic) PTSD. Rape is one of the most psychologically devastating things that can happen to a person, for example far more traumatizing than most military deployments. According to a 1992 study published in the *Journal of Traumatic Stress*, 94 percent of rape survivors exhibit signs of extreme trauma immediately afterward. And yet, nine months later 47 percent of rape survivors have recovered enough to resume living normal lives.

PTSD was once called shell shock or battle fatigue syndrome. It is a serious condition that can develop after a person has experienced or witnessed a traumatic or terrifying event in which serious physical harm occurred or was threatened. PTSD is a lasting consequence of traumatic ordeals that cause intense fear, helplessness, or horror, such as a sexual or physical assault, the unexpected death of a loved one, an accident, war, or natural disaster.

I, myself, have experienced mild symptoms of PTSD during and after Operation Desert Shield and Operation Desert Storm from depleted uranium poisoning. The Iraqi Republican Guard was quite smart. They moved their burning tanks near US operations as close as they could, and the burning paint and smoke would obstruct the view of the soldiers. The soldiers inhaled this toxic chemical into their digestive system, and it was later called Desert Storm Syndrome or cases of PTSD today. After Operations in Iraq, we are dealing with several cases of soldiers with severe cases of PTSD including soldiers who did not deploy as well. I think once you fire a weapon down range at a target, you learn what you are capable of doing with a weapons system. In combat, when you are fired at from the enemy and hear, see, or feel bullets hitting you or going by you, you get this feeling inside your body that you will never every forget again. It is just like me learning the skill of firing artillery projectiles in training. We always love to hear them go out of the cannon tube and fly down range, but during combat operations or full engagements with a T-72 tank, it is a much different sound when it comes into your area. When you are that close to the battle lines and you hear this distinctive sound, you will never forget it. When you return from deployments, sudden bangs or loud crashes set you off or make you hide or go inside, causing people to look at you and wonder what is wrong with that guy or gal. PTSD is different for everyone. Some people can get over it, while there are people who cannot live this down. They live on the battlefield daily, and a war is going on in their mind constantly. It is a never-ending battle between them, and their mind telling them the war is still going on, and these people sometimes need special attention or hospitalization.

When I went to deployments, I always had a thought with me. Dorothy said it best, "*There's no place like home*" because live or die I knew I was always going home alive or in a box. So far I have been following the yellow brick road, and I have not been to the magic kingdom yet or met the Wizard, but someday we will all meet him. Dealing with my PTSD, I have to deal with other issues as well. For now I'll list two:

Bio-polar: Bipolar disorder, the larger condition that includes bipolar depression, is a lifelong, or chronic, illness. It's a condition that affects the brain in a way that can cause extreme mood swings that vary in length. People with bipolar disorder can go from mania (the highs), feeling euphoric or revved up and irritable, to depression (the lows), feeling down or hopeless. These highs and lows are called episodes.

Anxiety: Anxiety is an emotion characterized by an unpleasant state of inner turmoil, often accompanied by nervous behavior, such as pacing back and forth, somatic complaints, and rumination. It is the subjectively unpleasant feelings of dread over anticipated events, such as the feeling of imminent death. Anxiety is not the same as fear, which is a response to a real or perceived immediate threat. Whereas anxiety is the expectation of future threat. Anxiety is a feeling of uneasiness and worry, usually generalized and unfocused as an overreaction to a situation that is only subjectively seen as menacing. It is often accompanied by muscular tension, restlessness, fatigue, and problems in concentration. Anxiety can be appropriate, but when experienced regularly, the individual may suffer from an anxiety disorder.

I've been to outpatient treatment and almost lost everything. I had to prove that I was capable of keeping my status because I had this dreaded disease. We as warriors or just normal people with an everyday job can get this from just about anything. Every day and every night I have to take a set number of prescribed pills, and I hope that I am a better person. There are times when the medications seem to make it worse because I think it has to do with the mood and type of situation and environment you are in. The other day I was at the VA and I was in one of the PTSD moods where I just wanted to see my counselor and be heading home because I had run out of a certain prescription over the week. You have some veterans who just will not leave you alone and will talk to you until you talk back ⁊ them. There was a guy who would not leave me alone. I felt very sorry for the guy because I was just sitting looking at my phone and listening to him having a conversation with himself. It's sad that we leave people alone like this and ignore the situation because lots of these veterans have nothing to go home to. This guy was in a full conversation with himself. He stopped and began talking to me. I was wondering who he was talking to. Then I realized he was speaking to me. I really didn't know what to say except hello and ask if he was speaking to me because I did not know his situation. I use this guy as an example because this person could have been me. It's as if people don't care about these veterans or they forget our veterans. People don't care if they served or not because PTSD is a hidden disorder. I would like to stress that though veterans may be home, they are suffering the aftereffects of battle fatigue and sickness. Please help someone with Post-Traumatic Stress Disorder (PTSD).

SAM007

TRANSITION

As an active duty service member with twenty years of honorable service, I feel I have done my duty and served my country proudly, even though I think I should have stayed for the long haul. If I had, maybe today I would be the Command Sergeant Major I dreamed I would be, or then again, I could have been killed. Where would I be today if I had stayed in the United States Army? I did my time at the Warrior Transition Brigade at Walter Reed Army Medical Center in Washington, D. C. When I referred myself to the Mental Health Department for signs of Post-Traumatic Stress Disorder, I knew my military career was over and there would be no more deployments in my life. I think four combat tours and multiple deployments to the Middle East were enough, and in speaking with my wife, one more would have killed me. A man's got to do what a man's got to do for his family.

I was married to the military/Army for nineteen years. Now, I was also a newlywed, and we had our daughter. I just returned from Iraq in 2006 and from the book tour for the *Center of Army Lessons Learned*, and I had more than my share of deployments. It was time to make a change in my life because the person my wife met was going away and the person my wife loved was gone. That person was never coming back, and it was hard to tell her because after my daughter was born, I was a proud father, but I lost touch with the world and my wife. There was a darkness that came out in me, and I wanted no one around. I started losing touch with guys in the unit and the people around me as well as my job.

When I went to the Warrior Transition Unit (WTU), I participated in all kinds of mental counseling and fundamental classes with other veterans who were dealing with the same issues. As bad as I was, there were some patients worse off than I. I remember being in classes where we had to use colored markers to depict actions that were going through our minds at the time. A lot of the guys and gals used the color *red* to show pain and suffering that they experienced in their tours. Some of our classes were group discussions or charades. My transition out of the military, while I was in outpatient psychiatric, was very slow; and I hated it. There were nights I sat in my room and just stared at the wall because I was away from my family and I felt so alone. I did go to the gym, and I hated seeing people there violating their profiles, but that's life. Sometimes it reminded me of a funhouse or a crazy farm because every day was something different.

There were various ranks from Private through full bird Colonel in our group and even a female USMC recruiter who went through some crazy shit herself. Everyone was there for a reason, and we all heard everyone's stories. Occasionally, everyone broke down in our group as their stories were told. I have all the respect for all these people in my group even though some of the people didn't go into combat. I learned that Post-Traumatic Stress Disorder occurs in different ways and that is what I am trying to show in this book. To this day, we are still blind on what's going on with our veterans who are serving, who have served from land to sea, and the problems they face on the battlefield or in the classroom. PTSD is a real killer, and it is stopping us dead in our tracks. You can't imagine the paperwork that is required while transitioning out of the military. You would never believe it! Every day some information or some type of status is required. It is like standing in line until roll call and accountability has to be done. Boy, we had a shit load of hurt soldiers. I was shocked at the number of soldiers who became wounded warriors.

It seemed like I was always going to the same places and nothing was ever getting done. I had to report to a Full Bird Colonel (COL) who was retiring from service himself, and I knew he didn't give a crap about my status. So I basically had to make sure I knew what was going on for my own good. I had to make sure I was reporting to my so-called Staff Sergeant (SSG) Platoon Sergeant three times a day, while I saw others report only once a day. What kind of system is that, double standard? I wanted my rating, I wanted to go home, and I couldn't believe it took the process a year and a few weeks to complete. My counselor was an Indian doctor and very helpful but very hard to understand. I don't know how many times they changed my medication and the type of medication (I will cover in another part of the book). Some made me really sleepy while some kept me awake at night. I remember at night I reviewed the day's paperwork on all my medical status and I did not understand shit. I would spend hours on the computer looking up medical terms and definitions on my medical status with the types of medication and why I was on these meds.

One thing I did was start my resume while I was there. Everyone who was at the WTU was given a desktop computer in the room. I was online, learning how to develop a resume, but it really did not help me because I was not the best at reading and social media was not my thing. I listened to a lot of music while I went through my transition period. Being alone helped me find who I really was and things I did not know about myself. Things I did not understand about myself, why I did things to people that I was unaware of, and why I never looked back on why I did them. I thought about my career a lot and felt like a loser, someone who had been forgotten. I felt as though I was in a recycle center for soldiers, an old soldiers' home, like the one my dad used to talk about. And now I'm there. I never thought I was going to see my little girl again. Then one day we were told that if we lived within a certain mile radius, we could start driving home on the weekends. This started to help me a little bit, and I was happy to see my family. I was still not the dad I used to be because I was still going through this change that I didn't think I was ever coming back from. I knew the person I was, was gone, and my daughter was too young to understand that her daddy would never be the same. Her daddy was gone, and a new daddy was here to stay. My wife totally understood my situation, and she was heartbroken and ripped part. Her lover was gone. I don't think we were intimate like we once were upon my return home. The love was gone, and it is still gone to this day.

I noticed there were a lot of fun things to do, but because they were more focused toward the soldiers with physical injuries, I just was not interested in them. It was as though the veterans with PTSD were not put in the same group as the wounded warrior group and their special activities. At least that's the way I saw it. If you were missing a leg or arms, you got really special treatment, and if you were in wheelchair, you got really special treatment because you could see their injuries. When you returned back with severe PTSD, your injuries were invisible and people didn't know that you were capable of committing suicide at any minute. Times are changing, and the military is taking better precautions for this. I just think some of this was not taken seriously, and I hated being bossed around by lower enlisted soldiers who didn't know their jobs and our current situations.

I think I found a light at the end of the tunnel when I was updating my resume and met some gentlemen from the Defense Department who were looking for a security intern for their agency and I fit the bill. I had an automobile, availability, they liked my resume, and they liked me. I started working downtown Crystal City in the Virginia/D. C. metro area. These guys took me by the hand and counseled me and mentored me in areas and different security areas. I was their first Wounded Warrior Intern, and I busted my ass every day, four days a week. I represented the United States Army the best I could, and my mentality was shifting more toward the civilian sector. My mentors were molding me this way. I wish I could mention their names, but I won't, though they were great leaders and mentors. The agency is a super agency to work for, and if I ever asked, I am sure they would take me back in a heartbeat. Unfortunately, I just live too far from there now. I do have great recommendations from my mentor and trainer, and my resume will always be top-notch because of people like him. I think to this day the reason I got that special call at the Crayola Factory when I was with my daughter and my wife is because these guys were networking with the government agency I work for now.

My transition from Walter Reed was still not the best. When I left Walter Reed, I was not in the best shape because I had to out process and go to a Transition Assistance Program (TAP). This program was a transition program jammed into one week. Two days of the program was resume writing with one day writing a resume and one day reviewing a resume. What a class! I really learned a lot, which placed me into a great job in the civilian world. The best thing I got from my twenty years in the Army was my MSM and a surprise from DOD when I was awarded the Joint Service Commendation Medal for service for serving one year at the Defense Department for Security. Wow! Not too many Field Artillery guys get a Joint service assignment for the end of their career and not too many FA guys get JSCM. I found myself driving back to the state of Pennsylvania with a job lined up with Pepsi Cola.

The worst job I ever had in my life and not one that a person with Post-Traumatic Stress Disorder should have was being a merchandiser for some twenty-nine-year-old boss. I thought the Army was bad with 0500 hours every morning meetings. I just lived down the street, but I was beat every morning. I was late getting out of work each night because I was slow at my job. Some of these guys worked circles around me. After a few months, I caught on, but after my experience in a WAL-MART with a manager whose company says they support veterans, I had to call it a day and hang up that job. I needed to look for better opportunities.

Let me explain. We in the cola world are to work as a team. I won't use the brand names, but I had soda in the back of the Wal-Mart stock area where we stored the soda and this other company area was a mess. I made sure our area was to the standard. I was used to that because of being in the military. I set the standard, and the manager was impressed with me. He asked me to be a team player, to set up the other cola exhibit, and clean up the soda area before I left for the day. I called my management, and I complained, but was told to follow the instructions of the manager because the manager runs the store. I told them I would be late to my other stores, and they told me I would be "written up." I tried to explain to the manager of the store, and he started yelling at me. I explained to him that I was a veteran with PTSD, and he laughed at me. He called my company, and they told me to keep my comments to myself or I would be fired. I explained to them at the next meeting that this company and WAL-MART do not support veterans with disabilities. I was leaving and I would never support their product again. I returned their crappy uniforms and T-shirts, dumped the posters, and everything they gave me and told the young manager he needed to get some people skills.

Life for me in the civilian world was a hard transition. I would come home at night a deadbeat dad and then have to take care of my daughter. My wife and I were not getting along. She constantly told me that I was a loser father. I was trying to manage the money, knowing my military retirement is barely paying for our house payment and no money left at the end of our pay. Now I have to tell my wife I quit my job at the cola company. I hate Pepsi so much that I never put them on my resume because I was embarrassed to say I worked for them. I probably never would be hired if anyone knew I worked for them as a merchandiser.

I got into law enforcement through a job I saw listed on USAJOBS.com. I applied for it and was selected to take the physical fitness test. All I could think about was the dreaded PT test in the military. I had to drive all the way to Pittsburg, Pennsylvania, for the test at the end of August 2008. It was really hot. When I got there, I only had a few minutes to rest because they called everyone in the room for push-ups. Man, I hadn't done this event since the Army, and I was not sure if I was going to pass due to having gained a little weight. I don't remember how many push-ups I did, and it was a pass-or- fail event. They counted to themselves. Then it was the sit-up event, which was a different way than the way I did it in the Army. We only had to lift our shoulders as fast as we could to our chest. I think that was much harder, and I knew I wasn't doing well in that event. It was also a pass-or-fail event with them counting to themselves. The next event was a two-and-half-mile stationary bike. I have been a PT stud and ran the two-mile run under thirteen minutes. For this event, I don't remember the time, but it was the hardest riding event I ever had to do, and I made it. I remember the guys and girls cheering me on as I rode this shitty bike that looked like no one rode in years. The building was out in the middle of nowhere, and sand was all around the building. If you passed, you received a letter in the mail. I drove home from Pittsburg hoping I could get in the Pennsylvania Department of Corrections Academy (DOCA). Five days later, I got the letter telling me to report to Elizabethtown, Pennsylvania, on October 1, 2008, for recall 0500 in the morning for urinalysis. That began Basic Training phase II all over again. I had put on more weight since leaving the Army, and this time we were running the show as it was all peer evaluation. We had a group Sergeant, but they were there to guide us. We did everything else.

DOCA was just the start of my security career. I just want to say it has been a ride. After I graduated from the Training Academy, I became a Correction Officer Trainee at the prison. Let's go back to day one at DOCA. I won't mention any names because I don't want to get anyone in trouble. If you read my book, you'll know who you are. First, we picked squad leaders to run the squads and a first class sergeant. Man, I wanted no part of this crap. So the class drew names, and people were asked to leave the room. Guess what? I happened to be the last name drawn because I served in the military for twenty years. After fifteen minutes, we all walked into the classroom and all the squad leaders were selected. It is down to four people—me and this other guy who I didn't really think was leadership material but some thought he was. The next thing I know I'm picking my team leads. I was selected to represent the class 01–06 as the Class Leader. Let me tell you, I have made some mistakes in my life but being the Class Leader in a training academy or group leader was a big one. When your people make mistakes, you take the hit and I mean you take the hit! Hey, I got a really cool T-shirt to prove it. All of the classmates pitched in and made a super cool student shirt with my name at the top. I was shocked that I was selected. It proves that people with Post-Traumatic Stress Disorder can accomplish goals they set in life. I never thought I would make it through the training academy after Walter Reed because of the pills I took have taken a lot out of me and the crap I've been through, but come graduation day I made it. I didn't do it alone. My class worked as a team to help everyone through this. My wife wasn't even there to see me walk the stage, and she didn't congratulate me for doing a great job.

Then life began at the Department of Corrections (DOC), an undisclosed location, for fear of retribution in what I have written on the next few pages. I am not sure if all DOCs are like this, but if you served in the military or you're coming out of DOCA in a leadership position, you are a target. That's what I felt like as soon as I walked in the door because it was a foreign language there and it was a four-letter word every time they called my name. I thought being prior Army I would be in the door, but in that system, you have to gain the respect from COs and Officers before anyone came to your level. You were treated like inmates really, and the inmates were nicer to you than the staff. Now I wasn't an inmate lover! That's what they called them at DOC. I learned a lot from the old timers and who to trust and who not to trust in my short time of about a year on staff. I guess I was cross-trained in all areas and even in Level 5 with the bad ones. I even worked with the crazy inmates who really had problems and needed to be locked-up and off the streets. My wife called me crazy when I came home at night from this job. I wanted to bring her in there one night to show her how I busted my ass to put food on the table and I'm not even a CO yet. I wasn't really cut out for that job because with PTSD I think it just got worse and my counseling at the VA was not very good. I would tell my doctor stories about things that happened to me in the prison. He told me this was affecting me badly, and it was going to catch up with me. It was already catching up at home with my kid and my wife.

Soon I was to graduate to Correctional Officer Trainee Level IV, but on a rainy Sunday afternoon I got the break I was looking for, for years. I got a strange phone call from a gentleman who worked for the Department of Defense. It's like they had been watching me for months or years because this guy knew everything about me. He was reading everything off my so-called resume I created some years ago. I was *jaw-dropped*! He asked me, "Are you ready for a new beginning and second retirement with the Federal Government?" I was so shocked, and he asked me when I could start. I was speechless and said I had to give DOC two weeks' notice for a good reference.

So I went back to tell DOC I was resigning my position as Correctional Officer Trainee and told them I'm going to work my specialty, Physical Security, and they laughed at me. They put me on the worst duty possible in the prison. It was Cross-Walks for two weeks and while I worked that crappy position, I caught an inmate trying to transport illegal substances from one side of the jail to the other through my checkpoint. There was a lot of material on the inmate. Well for that, I was well known at the prison and some of the COs came to me and told me I had done a good job and they were sorry I was leaving. I guess I earned their *respect*. I was asked to stay, but I didn't agree with the things that go on in the system. I'll never have someone tell me when I come to work that, "You'll be working here all night, like it or not!" I didn't have a choice due to other guards having bids in because they had been there longer than me.

Now I work in an environment with a great group of people who first helped me build my resume to a super product and then gave me the confidence to be the person I am today. I am freely open to them about my story and PTSD because it's important to me. I can come to work and know I have a job tomorrow. No one is going to drill me out of a little study book I have to carry with me, and I don't have to worry about an inmate taking my life. My job requires me to ensure that the people I work for are well protected by our national security as they work every day. I can do my eight hours and go home, but if my boss needs me I'll stay. I know I can go home and not worry about my PTSD getting out of control because I work in a stress-free environment. It has taken me a long time to climb the mountain, but I've done this without my family because I was always supporting them while I was suffering with PTSD and other problems. I have other health issues I have not addressed in my book, and I wish not to address because this book is about my Post-Traumatic Stress Disorder. Climbing the mountain is a difficult climb, but I have proven to others who do not believe in me that dreams do come true. I went from a kid who had to walk to school every day and never had a car in the family, to a skateboarder, to a young man who joined the US Army, participating in four combat tours and multiple deployments worldwide, to a father of a great little girl, and now protecting our people from the security threats at work. I hope someday to be a world-famous author of this book. Everybody's transition is different.

My God, my kid, my health, and my job are the most important things in my life.

SAM007

HEALING STAGES OF A MENTAL DISORDER

One of the roughest times I remember is when I was dealing with my demons and Post- Traumatic Stress Disorder (PTSD), when I had no treatment, when I punched walls until the blood came from my knuckles, and you couldn't even have a conversation with me. I was in a bad world, and I wrote about a bunch of bad shit. On the following pages I am going to share my writer's block and a set of poems that I have collected over the years. Without these poems there would be no "*mirror*" in which to reflect. It has taken me a great deal of time to locate this set of stories and group of poems, but they are an extremely important piece to my book. I think this is the section where the coping process begins and the time when you have all sorts of different disorders in your life. If you're one of the veterans or subjects out there who are dealing with this situation, please understand that I am still going through what you are now going through and it's okay. I wrote this book to help people like you and me. I too have suffered and spent my time at the Warrior Transition Unit (WTU) at Walter Reed Army Medical Center in an Outpatient Psychiatric Program. These times were hard for me as I was alone and trying to reach out to the world to find myself. I was trying to figure out if there was a key to the puzzle because I had no clue what was going on with my life. I felt as though I was in a cardboard box and there was no escape. I even had the cool drugs to go along with it, but they were controlled. As time went by the drugs wore off. I started finding myself and began counseling and taking classes that made me realize that I wasn't alone in this horrible nightmare. I met others in my group who were going through the same experiences.

I think for a short time I stopped writing my poems because I was so busy with classes and counseling. I was trying to better myself, and I was so exhausted at night that all I wanted to do was sleep. There was really no *happy* place for me until they told me that I was able to go home and see my family. That too was not the best because I was a changed person and a bit of a stranger to my family. Yet I looked forward to getting away from the WTU, being on my own, and driving back home to see my daughter. Sometimes seeing my wife made my condition worse, and I cannot explain it to you to this day because the effects are the same way even now.

I have reviewed all my poems and put them in an order to help you understand and to maybe set a path in your life that you can follow. I'm not saying I'm a *God* or the Anti-Christ, but I think some of my words and poems can help people recover from the craziness that is inside. A lot has gone on throughout my life, and I have seen the fear and death of the battlefield. Before the Army, I dealt with a very bad childhood. I was always wondering if I was going to get the strap when I came home from school or if my dad had made a new name up for me when I walked in the door. I joined the Army to get away from all that nonsense. Enlisting into the Army at only nineteen, walking right in a combat zone, with deployment after deployment—it all took a toll on me. The experience changed me, and I could not control the anger anymore. So I reached out for help, which meant giving up the best thing I knew that was near and dear to my heart. I gave up my career in the military.

So if you're feeling suicidal or you have a bad case of a mental disorder, I hope my book finds you and your inner self to provide some help before it is too late. My collection of words and wisdom is a dedication to all who served this country and who have put everything on the line for something or nothing. You might be a veteran with PTSD, a hurting spouse with nothing left, or a service member who likes to read and enjoy a good book. This book is focused on retirees who have lived the long road and who are looking for a cure to some terrible mental killer that we call Post-Traumatic Stress Disorder. It is killing millions of veterans every day because they try to reach out but no one is there to help. I hope that one or two of my stories are heard or read by someone hurting out there and that it helps to relieve a bit of sadness or pain.

SAM007

THE PEOPLE IN THE MIRROR

In the morning, I wake up and rub my eyes, and I move toward the bathroom to take a glance in to the mirror. "Hello!" I see this crazy guy standing in front of this mirror. I think about the people who try to be someone else they admire. For me, everyone is on the other side of the mirror in a world that only I can control because of the darkness and pain on that side. If I break through this mirror, I will see you through the cracks of it. I study your each and every move you make. I want to see what you're about. If I see something I like, I go for it. I make that magical move toward you. If not, I pick up and place each and every piece one by one back into the solid position of the frame and my power makes the mirror whole again. You will be stuck in my world!

The frame will never break again because it will be held together by this bond; it's like a bunch of dead little souls holding everything together. When I'm finished, I will break your soul and start all over again with another mirror person. People in the mirror are alike one way or another because they like to hurt, cause pain, and pick on others around them. We all have a shiny and dull side. As I look out through the mirror at you, I can see your hurting and the pain that you are feeling. We all come in many shapes and different colors. Some stick out, and some hide from others. Like the mirror, they are all fragile and our feelings can get hurt at any time. Standing inside this mirror, I can see this every day. People don't understand that they break mirrors every day. They just go on with their lives like nothing ever happens, so give yourself to me and step into my world where someday you will be one of my mirror people.

SAM007

THE MANY PAGES OF A BOOK

The many pages of a book tell a story about someone or something. The pages that are found beyond this page talk about the many experiences and feelings that I felt at the time. Hidden away in these pages are very short stories and sad poems. Also, there are some very long stories about the past and the future. Each and every page is different in every way. No two pages are alike in any way. You will see from reading the many pages, there had to be a story to tell or it would be hidden forever.

You may ask yourself, "How was this to be?" Most of the pages deal with dreams, combat, or relationships between people. You might not get anything out or this and go on with your day or you may shed a tear or two. The word needs to get out because if I had never written anything down, I guess you might think I am some kind of *nutcase*. All of this pain, but why? Being only twenty-six years old, a young sergeant in the US Army and not knowing if I'd have a job the next day was a frightening experience. I will never forget the combat zone where I saw the dead along the road and I did what I was told to do. Now after combat/war, I returned home to see my family and losing a woman because of the dumb decisions I made for her and my friends. For the families we killed in combat in the Middle East with artillery, I'm sorry for killing you and taking you from your families. It was my job in which I was given an order, and as a soldier, I will follow my last instructions given to me as trained.

Now you know the story of a young twenty-six-year-old, living in fear day to day in this man's Army. There is a lot to be told on the next few pages of this book. In the end, you will feel the darkness I went through. The pain I will never forget, a pain you can't see because it is hidden within my walls.

Now open your mind and let yourself go and come in into my world. Enjoy page after page after page.

SAM007

LIVING ON THE RAZOR'S EDGE

Playing with life because you have nothing left.
You go faster and faster, so fast that you don't want to stop.
The only thing that will stop you is the object that you hit next.
Always taking a chance because nothing ever happens to you.
Just waiting for death and time to both meet you in the right place,
And then you rest and play these little games no more.

All that will be left is the hurting and the pain you left in someone's heart.
You're like a cat with nine lives and soon everything will be on top of you.
Then you'll have no place to hide.
In the end you're out on a limb and soon it will break.
Then your dream will come true.

Always talking about being on the razor's edge and killing yourself,
Just keep doing wrong and going faster and faster and you meet
    death face-to-face.
For now you ride the Razor's Edge.
Your time door is closing, so wake up and get on the right track
    because if you don't.
Someday I'll be reading this to your tombstone.
Then the world will be quiet and you'll look down on your grave,
And wish you had never lived on the razor's edge.

SAM007

PTSD INSIDE AND OUTSIDE
OF THE FAMILY

I'm not going to write much about my childhood, but from this and understanding why people have Post-Traumatic Stress Disorder (PTSD), you might start figuring out the puzzle. Growing up in the Stephens' household was not the best way to grow up. I won't disclose a major part of my private life, but what I'm writing about will shock you and other readers. When you have PTSD, sometimes you say things that you don't mean. You say things to family members that you never wished that you said, but it's too late and the damage is done, and you can't take back what you said. When someone or something sets you off, it's as though a killer takes over your mind.

My whole life I grew up locally and never traveled anywhere outside of Pennsylvania. I grew up in a middle class family with one sister who was kind of slow at education and learning things. She was in the Special Education Program at school and was until she graduated from a so-called school and continued living at home until many years later, living off my parents.

My parents worked at the local carpet factory. My mother packed skids, and my dad did odd jobs like truck driving. They tried to make the best for us as a family or what I thought was a family. I was always fighting with my sister and hearing my mother and father fighting as well. This story really goes back to when my father started drinking and smoking every day and calling my mother names that I won't repeat in my book. For years and years I put up with my father calling me a *creep* and *bum* and beating me with a leather belt whenever he felt like it. I was never known as son or Billy. It was strange because my mother let him do it, and as a young kid I never could understand why. I guess my dad was *"the boss,"* and he would put my mother in her place if she was out of line. So I went through life and high school daily as my father called me these names. My friends made fun of my family and basically called them *the Monsters*. I don't know if this was a slight PTSD setting in, but boy, I really needed to get out of this situation before I become a loser like my family.

For years I saw my sister feed off my parents and I thought, *Do I really want to become this, or do I want to be something and make a name for the Stephens family?* I look back on the history of my name, and there are not too many famous people listed. So I told my parents good-bye, and I joined the Army for the best of all of us because I wanted to make something of myself. I joined the Army, and boy, was I wrong! I walked right into a combat operation that changed my whole perspective toward the Army. After several combat tours, getting to see the world, and retiring after twenty years, I honorably closed that chapter.

Now I have little nine-year-old who thinks the world revolves around her. If she only knew the stories that my dad put me through when I was a child, she would totally understand but maybe someday she will. Right now she thinks Pappy Bill is the greatest man because he's old and he gives her money. It was the same with Grammy Sue until she died, and then I had to beg her to come out and visit her grave with her pappy. I'll never forget all the crap that my dad put me through, but now he is alone without anyone. I am at his side today, and I am the only one he has left in his life. He does not drink or smoke anymore. We don't talk about the old times; we just talk about the future. Pappy Bill is also there if my family needs something, but they don't seem to understand that. My little one hardly comes to visit him, and I think it is because of her mother. Don't even get me started on that one. She hasn't even been to my mother's grave except maybe one time since she died. My daughter is in competitive cheer and pageants. She is a winner in a lot of her events. I am very proud of her, but she always wants more. I have tried to step in and control this situation. Sometimes I have to draw the line, and there are things I say that I don't want to say. Again my Post-Traumatic Stress Disorder kicks in, and I am so glad I am not a drinker or a smoker to make the situation even worse. I sometimes yell at the top of my lungs at my wife and daughter because there is no control, and she just doesn't stop. My wife digs and digs, and she doesn't see it. You think because you can do a bunch of flips and rolls and have a bunch of trophies and ribbons you are some fairy-tale princess, but you are not. When I was a kid I never played any sports. I never earned a trophy or one single ribbon for anything. Still your mom lets you play with your awards like toys, you break them up, and soon you'll have none. Then you throw these little, tiny fists about things not going your way, and soon you set me off. It is really nothing, and you really have no say so in this whole situation. When I was kid, I had no say and no limit on anything. You have so few limits and freedom that you would be shocked if you knew how I grew up.

PTSD is truly in our family, and I am not sure if it started in my childhood or on the battlefield. I'll tell you what, it will be a part of your life if you want to be a part of my life. Every day we hear family members are dealing with the same problems as I am and some worse than my situation. Some can't be helped. Sometimes the veteran takes his/her life or the spouse ends their life over the stressful situation in the household. I just want you to understand that I know my daughter goes to school wondering what's wrong with her daddy. I'm glad she can go to school and not be called *creep* or *bum* for the rest of her life. I will always be scared in my mind for my daughter. When I look at her, it always reminds me how happy I am to tell my father the accomplishments she has done day after day and year after year. Now the book has closed in his chapter in life because Pappy Bill is gone forever and she know he is gone. I heard her say, "Now that He's gone there must not be any more Santa Claus because he's gone." There's a time in life where we come to that crossroad and must make a decision in life. We pick heaven or hell that our Creator has chosen for us. He lived a good life, and I hope he's happy because he's now with my mother.

SAM007

LOCKED BEHIND THE DOOR

Looking into your heart I can see the darkness. It's like the angel of death herself looking back at me. You're on a path that you follow day after day because of the problems in the past. You are scared for your life in blood and soul. Your juices follow with the passion, but you're filled with the poison like a snake waiting to strike at any time. Your sexual desire burns within your soul that you can't control…a desire that no one can describe. Something you hide from this world because of a curse that was inflicted upon you from that day. Waiting for a miracle from *God* or could it be that bright burst of energy to break this spell.

Trapped!

Trapped, in a world of your own. A man you have known for a very short time figures out your pain and hurting that you are going through. He can feel what you are feeling because he can read the thoughts in your mind. Waiting and waiting, you want to give yourself to him. A wall that you have built around yourself like a barrier. This stands between you two. You look at him, and he looks at you. You both are feeling the power held deep within your hearts. Now knowing the secrets that you hide from him, what can you do? You soon close your eyes and begin to cry and imagine sexual passion you both could be encountering.

Waking up, you find yourself in your own puddle of your lust, and then he's gone.

SAM007

FORGOTTEN ADDICTION

Here we have a situation between two people are trying to build something they never had. To build something that should have started from the bottom and went to the top…a relationship without a foundation. No bricks or stones just a magical drug we call *sex*, a tool that we use for pleasure and control. A drug we can't control becomes an addiction. It's something that will not stop us because of this intense feeling that we get from it. Always wanting more and more, we can't stop it from driving us out of control. We are lost in our own emotions, pretending to be something that we are not. A drug you can't let go of because how good it makes us feel inside.

Addicts we are because of this driven force between us. Calling my name and listening to you going into another world. Soon you will have to return from this magical trip, and there is nothing and no feeling. The drug is worn off. You need it again and again to make you happy.

I will never forget how good it was but now we must try to forget; forget the pain that we put each other through. Something keeps me here, but what is it? Is it that four-letter word that we don't like to use? Every day there is this thought of this addiction that I must forget about and can never use again because of where it may lead us in the future. Maybe this habit needs to stop? Maybe this is a problem we just can't see or we are both blinded by the light. Without this we are nothing. Waking up from your magical trip you begin to see the light, a light that was never there. A light we had to create because we had to. Just like screwing in a light bulb or a candle with no wick and a bunch of melted wax all over it. An addiction that must stop before it is too late. You're killing me, and we are killing each other the more and more we stay in this together. Wishing this would have worked and went somewhere and could have gone somewhere.

Dragging you from your significant other and catching you with one hand. I stole your soul and took your heart from him. Just to end this because of this habit I will never have control of this. Always wanting more and more and never enough and not even you can give enough of what I want. This is the way it will be until I find the right path.

"Building a bridge is hard to do when you don't have the supplies, but burning it down is much easier when you hold the match to the fire."

Another page added to the never-ending tale of life.

SAM007

PEOPLE OF THE FALLEN NIGHT

Nighttime is coming faster and faster as I watch the last of the clouds end this quiet but sad day. The air is cool, and the wind is at a standstill. The sky is beginning to get darker and darker. The moon begins to peak over the mountains, shadows start to take form. There are people in the streets seen looking and gathering food. Children without parents are trying to find a love one. Only at night they walk, trying to solve the untold stories about the ones that are missing. The ones who go out at night and never come back. The voices are fading into the walls where they once came from before. At night, while you are walking, you hear footsteps behind you. You turn to see what it could be, but it's nothing! There's something and someone out there lurking. You're always being watched day and night. They watch your every move that you may take. These people or sprits hide in your dreams.

There waiting for you to slip in your dreams, the night traps you. There's no way out of this trap. Just wake up. Someone is always waiting to fill your slot because you will be dead, and this will start all over again.

There's no telling what will happen to you. A lot of the times when you slip, you will become a part of the frozen wall of thoughts and visions. Don't ever let your dreams take control of you. Too much control may cause you to become one of the people of the fallen night. So watch your step in your dreams.

SAM007

THE BLACK KNIGHT

There once was a story written, and many believed it was true. This story dates back to the early pioneers and Dark Ages. This is how it was told.

> Whenever he was seen as riding his evil black horse, he looked very powerful in the darkness. At night when the light was just right, his armored shined bright against the moonlight. He sat on the hilltop looking down into the tiny village, looking for that perfect moment that he could take a lonely woman. He never made a sound as he moved through the night. If you were close enough, you could hear his hollow, death heartbeat pounding. His horse would breathe fire and smoke. When the clouds were just right and the moon set just right, you could look yonder and see his shadow fading into the spooky fog. As the Black Knight rides, you could see the redness of his horse's eyes through the dense fog.
>
> You could tell the Black Knight held the power of all the other nights throughout the kingdom and the land. Moving like a train ready to jump the track at any time. I've never seen anything so fast as that before in my life. Now heading toward the tiny village, knowing something was about to happen was a woman in his death path craving a blood bath.

The story is written to this day that the Black Knight is still on the rampage looking, and just maybe...

If you're not careful, he just might catch up with you, so watch out! As the old story is told more and more and books of this tale are written and the days get longer and longer the Black Knight is out there. The more he kills, the stronger and stronger he gets.

SAM007

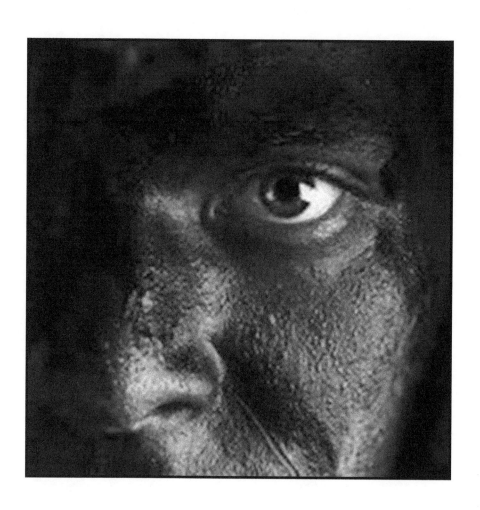

WHAT IS MY PURPOSE IN LIFE?

Here I am away from it all.
Here I am away from you. Here I am waiting for you to call.
Here I am waiting without a clue, just waiting for you.
The days are long waiting for you.
What should I do?
Where should I go?
What is my purpose?
Why won't you come?
Sitting here, my mind is filled with crazy ideas thinking of things to do to you.
Trying to make you feel wanted.
Trying to make you feel at your max.
Trying to make you feel the best you've ever felt before.
How can I do this?
Sometimes, I think I'm just a bore.
Sometimes, I think what is my purpose in life?

SAM007

NO MORE FEELINGS

One day, as I was walking down this magical road of life, I came upon the dear pagan. "Oh, Pagan," I said. I talked to the pagan and explained to him that everything was so wonderful. I was feeling super and on top of the world. About this time in my life I totally opened myself to this special someone, but how special really was she to me? These things I had never done or felt before. These things I will never do again for anyone as long as I live.

As the relationship got deeper and deeper, I felt pain deep down in my heart, a pain I've never felt before.

What must this be?
I asked myself.
To this day, I can't understand the pain I felt.
I can still feel the pain inside pulling me down.
What can I do about this pain?
Should I just end this wicked love game?

Can I wake up from this terrible dream or can I reach into the sky to turn this all around to what this used to be?

It has been some time since I have heard anything from her, that voice.

Where could that voice have gone?

What will ever happen if we ever meet face to face again?

Something so strong, did not last so long.

Ending in this sad song, thinking you have it all and you're on top of the world.

Soon you come to reality and wake up from that miserable dream, and you have nothing.

A relationship that went nowhere, my feelings are fading more and more each day as we are apart. That's all it was, just a short roller-coaster ride, up and down; and now there's nothing because everything has stopped and turned to stone.

SAM007

HOW SHORT LIFE IS

A man in a busy world works and lives day to day. The streets downtown are busy, and crime is the thing he worries about. The sky is starting to get dark, and the mood begins to change. The streetlights come on, and everything is starting to get wild around him. Everything is moving faster than the speed of light and sound itself. It's now midmorning, and the streets are dark and empty. All you can hear is a cat digging through a trash can. As the end of this day nears, a new day is to follow soon behind. The man begins to move back to his room, still dazed from the last night's activities. As he enters the room he notices a white balled-up object on the desk by the lamp. The man clears his head and begins to read the note. He finds out that his girl can't stand to be with him any longer.

The man begins to think to himself as thoughts race throughout his mind. He thinks, *What did he do to deserve some kind of news like this from the woman he loved so dear?* Sitting in his own world of hurt the man knows there is nothing to do but go on with life or end it all.

Life starts all over just like that day-to-day thing. How short is life really.

SAM007

TURNING YOUR BACK
IS HARD TO DO

There you stood among the crowd. As I stood in the dissonance staring at you, I could feel this bright serge of energy moving throughout my body. Your movements just filled my mind with the many ideas and things that I always wanted to do to you in the past. I knew on this night, I have found the one but why because I was soon to leave to another place. I thought to myself as we talked. Sometimes people meet just for one thing. This was different because I saw the creativity within her soul. I read her every thought she was thinking. I could sense the darkness that she was holding within her heart and didn't want to speak about.

I saw you as more than just a sex object. For just a short time I have known you, and it feels like forever. She is a woman who is in her own world with a style that I can't describe. Looking into her eyes, I could see that something is there, but it's locked deep within the doors of her mind. It's so sad to say, "That I had to meet a goddess who needs a king." I really wish that I could be that king. Doing what I must, I have to turn away and bow my head from something I want so badly. Time ticks and ticks away as nobody knows when our time clocks will stop. Just another dream that I wish that had come true. Closing my eyes, I walk away and fade into the darkness.

SAM007

BULLET TO THE BRAIN

You're standing in a room with a candle burning low.
In one hand you're holding a revolver with one bullet in the chamber.
You're playing the game.
One shot, one kill.

In the other hand, you're holding a rose; the petals are falling off one by one.
She loves me, she loves me not.
This is a love game.

So! What is your choice?
The bullet in the brain
         or
The woman who drove you insane?

SAM007

THE ROOM THAT TOOK HER AWAY

A girl sits in a squared off room with a small lit candle at her side. The darkness is creeping around her, like death itself. Waiting and waiting for the perfect chance to see her when she least expects it.

One speaker radio plays in the distance, and the small girl walks to the fourth floor window and glances out to see nothing but a very faint star burning in the sky. Her heart is pounding about to come out of her chest. It's like it could skip a beat at any second. The visions that she is depicting in her mind are visions that won't go away.

Now looking beyond life itself, everything good is gone. This is all just one big blur in her troubled mind. Her mind is blank, like the walls in the room.

No friends, no loved ones, and no family.

Pain is everything she feels.

There's no tomorrow.
"Today is it," said the girl.
She was gone!
Never to be seen again, her story is true because it is about you.
Everything I quit in a small dark room.

SAM007

DREAM RIDER

As I ride, I sit on my horse and think of you.
Riding into the night, I begin to cry with your picture on my mind.
I can see a Goddess of light.
Will you always be in my heart?
If I live or if I die?
The dream rider rides and rides
and rides, and then he dies.

SAM007

MOMENTS BEFORE I DIE

It's, oh, dark hundred hours; and it almost time for guard duty. I try to wake up my battle buddy for the next shift. He is not responding because he is caught in his own dream world. I tell him, "I got your six," and you're covered for the night. I knew on this night there should have been two of us on duty because I had this butterfly feeling in my stomach. As the sky got darker and darker, my movements got slower and slower. I started to worry, and the movements around and what was in front of me. Standing here, everything felt like the world had stopped for that few seconds and turned to stone.

Then suddenly!

I felt this cold hole ripping my side wide open. As I looked over, I noticed I was standing in my own puddle of blood. I noticed my partner was not moving as well as his last dream faded away into the darkness as he bled. The whole world seemed to flash right before my eyes before I had been shot again and again. I felt bullet after bullet breaking me apart. Waiting for death to take me at any time because of this mistake I made on this night.

So remember, use the buddy system; it could save your life someday.

SAM007

THE SECRET WALL OF DARKNESS

Sitting on this wall, I am looking out and about. Thinking of the times we shared at this spot together. Our feelings we collected at this wall, just you and me. A castle we built together so strong. Nothing can break these stonewalls down. Only you and I control how the wall is built. The sun shines bright on each and every brick that was laid in place. At night the stars shine so bright, so high in the sky. Like the mighty gods watching down on us. The wind blows against the walls in the darkness.

Everything is gray at the wall without you. Watching and waiting to see if you will ever return to the wall, to sit here beside me on this broken old raggedy bench. Never to bring another soul to this vey spot we cherish because this wall is for us to laugh and cry and to express our deepest secret of darkness.

SAM007

BLACK FORMALITIES

Standing in the distance is a woman staring right back at me. I notice something about her. The black silk lace lines her breast and hugging her buttocks. Her black nylons seize her legs. They look very strong and very smooth. As I come upon this impressive dressed female, my eyes scan her from head to toe. She reaches out and touches my face. Her warm touch made me feel wanted before I could say anything. She pushes her firm body against mine. It's like clouds before a thunderstorm. I stood up and pushed her on this massive black bed. I began to venture over and about her body. I noticed as I looked at her body, not just what she was wearing was black, but everything around us was dark as well. She started pouring mixed drinks, a drink or maybe two, and I was through. I was in another world. A very dark world, my head began to spin and I fell in to a deep coma.

When I recovered, I found myself lying in a corner all balled up. I was in completed darkness, feeling around for anything I could get my hands on around me. I was in this room trapped beyond these walls. It was like someone threw me here, in this room, and locked the door and threw away the key forever.

Maybe this is just one big fairy tale? Then I realized while I was studying in my room, my eyes began to get heavy and I couldn't keep my eyes open any longer. I slipped and bumped my head on the desk and woke up. So remember, when you're caught in one of your own dream worlds, follow the light and you will find what you are looking for. Never go where the darkness is because you may be playing with your own life. In my world, you might get involved with your dreams, you just might die.

SAM007

SHADOWS IN THE CORNER

Out of the darkness you appeared from the large crowd, looking for something. But what?

Your spontaneous love style…You searched, located, and found what you were looking for. Sitting there as we talked about life and where this could go, I was thinking I was on this magical trip for a one-night stand. I didn't know if we were ever going to talk again or if this was going to be the night of my life?

All night you were just another shadow in the corner to me because I was not there for what you thought I was there for. My mind was playing tricks on me because of a small pain I felt in my heart. I was doing something wrong, but for the good. In the end, I saw the bad in this and wanted to continue my lust that I was feeling at the moment.

Now seeing the good and bad and happy and sad we have drawn a line between the two of us. I have pushed you away because you've made it this way. Nothing left, as we continue to climb this mountain. You and I together, as one, were sweating and doing something; but for what? I think for the thrill of the sex drive.

You're here one minute and gone the next, as I lay motionless in bed, thinking, *Oh, what a night!* We are no more because she left without looking back as she walked out the door. Strange as it seems we hardly talk anymore. Sometimes in the wee hours of the morning, I can see you on line but hidden, hiding within the numbers of social media, just like I like to do.

How's the weather? I need help with my MP3. I'm hoping that there is a plus with this? Never knowing the future or setting goals; we never planned because it was all about me and not even you. Knowing something she feels is good but sees the bad. Hoping I can change this space between us two. Lonely we both are, but afraid to show it and express it to each other.

The shadow of you is haunting me night after night. The scent of you will never go away as I once asked you to stay. The shadows of you are clinging to me as I try to see a plus and move on. Something tells me to stay and not to go away.

My lines are short and true because I have nothing left to do. Empty as I feel and hoping you do as well. Thinking because we must. I fell in love with you, and it was too late to tell.

SAM007

THE DREAM RIDER'S LAST RIDE

As I ride into the sunset, I ride along the horizon. Never knowing where I will stop. Only when my eyes grow heavy I will stop. For now there is no resting, and there is no pain. Riding into the darkness, not knowing what lies ahead of me. This might sound like some sort of game. Really, it is not. I've done this many times, but now it's time to stop because I am tired with life. I wish to go no longer.

Soon my ride will stop because I will die. The ride gets slower and shorter. Resting, I am waiting for you. Waiting for you to take my hand and join me. I am not going anywhere. So jump on and take a ride. It just might be your last ride. The rider's last cry. Now everything has stopped because the rider has died.

SAM007

REPLACE ME

I remember the days sitting here broken and all alone. Thinking back to the many times I'm left to do it all myself. There was no one, no help, just me and my shadow to accomplish the mission. When something had to be done, I was left to do it. I was left in in the spotlight. I'm not a movie star, so leave me alone. I'm not slave, so put your whip away. Sometimes that's what it feels like.

I'm a person!

I can only do so much; I'm going to break soon. I am not a machine, and I will break down. I will be replaced, and the process will start all over again. Others just sit back and watch and wonder what's going through my mind. As they look at me.

Someday, I'll stop!

Then they will all be lost in their own world, and nothing will get accomplished.

Everything will just fade away and die.

SAM007

A PUPPET ON A STRING

Here you sit in this workshop, waiting to be carved by the woodsmen. All you are is a block of wood with a hollow heart. Everything is moving around you. "Oh, how good it would feel to adventure out and see the rest of the woodshop," you asked yourself. Time passes, and you soon start to take form. You now have arms and legs, and you are no longer cold at night because now you even have clothes as well. Now you're starting to take form, and now you feel better about yourself.

The night comes; you start to hear new and strange sounds that you have never heard before. Trying to move out of this corner that you are in, you glance up to see the many strings running from all parts of your wooden body to nowhere. Only the Puppet Master can control your each and every move that you will make. Someone is controlling you. People don't think about this, but they are just like puppets on a string. Someone is always controlling their each and every move they make. By giving them instructions or demanding them to do something above their own free will. Maybe a military command or order we must follow. In the end, you're in control of yourself. You make your own decisions and follow your liable for your own actions.

SAM007

SEARCHING

Sitting here with my latte, drinking away,
Searching for the untold stories that we hide from this everyday world.
As we enter a new world, it's time to pray.
Searching night and day for the answers.
Searching for a clue from you.
Reading the many books halfway through, for something but what?
What to do?
Sitting here thinking of another line to say.
It's been sometime since I've written because I have been away.
Lonely without you.
Lonely without anything to do.
Walking in my shadow, talking to myself.
Looking in this mirror, wondering what to do.
Trying to find the perfect clue.
Where do I start?
Where does this end?
Night after night, I sit with this magical pen and write.
Searching.
Searching for what?
Searching.
Searching for a plus.

SAM007

CAUGHT ON THE WEB

Sitting here with my laptop, watching the screen, Window one minute and Netscape the next. Just sitting here in the dark, waiting and waiting for someone to come online. Never knowing who it will be or if a virus will in the end. I'm taking my chances as I surf the nightly web searching for you.

Then one day on ICQ you appeared. Are you male or female?
Waiting.
Then I began to smile as I noticed the words on my screen.
Just wondering if these words have a face or not.
Night after night we sit and chat for many hours, building a friendship without face.
Am I falling for a bunch of words on a screen from a computer?
Funny as it sounds, I think I am.
A computer?
Somewhere, but where?
Where are you and what you doing at this time?
What do you think at this moment?
Some night I'm lonely because you are not there with me.
Then there are other nights, I just can't turn you off because I am caught in this magical World Wide Web.
Like a spider waiting, building something, but what?
The images I have of you, are they real or a dream created by some computer chip?
Time will tell.
I'm waiting and waiting because I know that this person behind the keys on the other side is doing the same as me.
Waiting and waiting I want to give myself to you.

In the future, we made a commitment to step away from these keys and meet face-to-face in the real world.

Time.

Time is counting down and ticking away as we build this web between us two every day.

I have to hold it in and save it, expressing myself on these keys to you.

Where you go at night when we log off?

Are you asleep?

What are you thinking about?

Someone, but who? I hope it's me?

A distance that we both have between us two.

A distance that we must close.

A web we are both building day after day.

Sitting here watching my screen.

Waiting…Waiting…

"You have a message."

Then there's nothing!

SAM007

A FULL DECK

I'm sitting at the table with the devil, Satan himself. You look at him, and he looks you right in the eyes and tells you to "Draw." One by one we all pick our cards. We start out with a full deck, not knowing who will get the last card. Each card we receive is laid face down, which represents relationships. Playing because we must, this is all about life itself. Never knowing which card we will pick next. My deck is empty because of the pain which is inside, a pain that will never end. I'm always picking the wrong cards from the deck, causing the pain inside. Only the Devil himself can take this pain away from me. The game must go on. How many cards are left in your deck?

SAM007

BREAKING THESE CHAINS

Here I sit in this jail cell, wondering why I am here. Looking at my hands and feet, all I can see is a chain from the wall to myself. I notice a nasty smell in the air. Looking at the green mold on these pipes, now knowing how long I must remain here, wondering if I'm going to live or die in this hellhole. Sometimes looking into the sky I ask the Lord "to break these chains." When nothing happens or there is no answer from above, I know there is no one who can ever help me from the outside to get away. Hearing the voices and the screaming from an inmate just killed over a pen. The scent of blood is in the air. I know I should have never taken that old man's life over that bag of food the other day that I wanted so bad. "Can I break these chains?" From the look of my hands, I am just here and want to cry and say good-bye.

SAM007

MY ROYALTIES

As a teen, I look back to all the time I wasted, all those love letters passed in class, boxes of chocolate, and single-stem roses on all the forgotten souls of whose names I can't even remember. I look in an old yearbook to remember and think to myself, *That was Sally Sue?* There were times when I brought you to the United Stated to meet my friend after I came back from combat. All I thought about were material things and not even you. I dressed you up in the best clothes, and while in Korea for one year, I sent back all kinds of designer purses. What did you do? You gave them all to your friends, used me time after time, and slept with my friends. The situation was so bad. I had to get you intoxicated for you to tell me the truth. Still I was wrapped around your finger and would not let you go. I just kept buying you this and that…whatever I thought would make you happy. Our love was so strong, but why? I just could not figure it out. No separation, but why? Could you be that one? Could you be the special person to make that bond? You had other plans that I did not know of, and I was crushed when I returned from my next deployment. Our love was lost, but somehow we still survived as friends. We are more like brother and sister, hinting here and hinting there. You got payback when you found out that he was married and had another family. Then I was off to the "Land of Oz," where more was to come, more deployments, more darkness, and more haunting. This time I left you my materials things. What did you do? You used it all against me, and even tried to get credit in my name. You tried to destroy me and tried to hurt me while I was gone. When I returned, I returned to a different person, to a different world. Why was the world so against me? And what did I ever do to you? You were the one who was like a mentor to me, the one who gave everything to me, and now gives everything to her country. For some reason, I just could not get along with your son. There were other plans for you which included another great guy and his family who you're with today.

The biggest mistake I ever made in my life was marrying my wife. I gave you everything off my back. I gave you my love, my heart, and my soul. You've seen me through the good and bad. I saw you through the happy and the sad. You have seen my sides of the mirror; you know the truth of who I am. I know my darkest secrets and the things I would never say to anyone. For nineteen years, I gave my soul to the Army and heart to Military. When I met you, I melted and was created again. I knew that I was ready to settle down to begin a family. I never knew that I was looking into a mirror. It was just a spell that was cast on me for a short time, or have I fallen into a black hole forever?

Financially, everything with you was a bad choice. Ever since I have been with you, I have been in a hole that I cannot escape. When we married, your debt became my debt and that was difficult enough to handle. Next, we had our daughter, and I love her very much. However, ever since I wanted to be a dad, I wanted a boy because of my terrible childhood. I was never taught how to throw a football or a baseball by my father as a boy. I imagined how great it would be to teach my son these things. When we had a girl, my dreams were shattered as I did not think that our daughter would participate in sports. She is into cheerleading and pageants, which really takes a lot of time and money. It is my responsibility to make sure that the money is there for these events. The main reason I wrote about you is because you had the nerve to remove your diamond ring, the ring that I worked so hard to pay for, a bond for our marriage, and you just removed the ring from your finger for good one day. I continued to wear my ring like a jackass.

You have made me look at a woman in a different way. I look back at every little love letter, rose, chocolate box of candy, poem, movie, or dinner out and for what? For some kind of thank you? Where does my money go each month? Where does my VA or military retirement go each month? The only support you're going to get from me is for our daughter. You've all made me look like a fool, but no more. I might still be married, but

I am separated, and I will continue to find sources of pleasure. With my pleasure, they will understand I go *Dutch* or I don't go at all. My royalties are to be in the near future to get rid of you and to write this book for veterans. I hope to do very well in the publishing side of the house because there are things I would like to do. If my father is still alive, I will buy a new house for him and me while you remain in our current home with our daughter. You can drive your same vehicle until it breaks down as you have noted. You constantly say you want nothing from me and you'll get nothing from me because my royalties will be my royalties. I'll go where I want to go, buy what shirt I want to buy, and drive what I want to drive. No more control freak. I have enough to deal with—Post- Traumatic Stress Disorder and other emotional disorders in my life. I don't need your issues affecting my health and my lifestyle as I try to complete another chapter in my life. How about that box of chocolates I asked for?

SAM007

HOME-WRECKER

What I'm about to write is my true feeling on how I view my relationship with my wife. I served in the United States Army for twenty years and nineteen of them I was married to the military, and I truly believed "If the Army wanted you to have a family, they would have issued it to you." Don't get me wrong, I did support my soldiers' families. That's what made me a good leader, but my time was to come. I won't talk much about the boyfriend-and-girlfriend thing, but there sure were a lot of fun times we had, going to concerts and other cool things. Then I asked her to move in with me, into my little house I had in Carlisle, Pennsylvania. Now I did not know that she had skeletons in her closet, and I never asked her to disclose them to me. As soon as she moved in, things began to change around my place. Things began to be out of order and messy. She started making decisions around my place for me and not asking me. I would go away for long periods of a time for training, and when I returned, things would be different around the house.

What was I getting myself into? Was I falling for the chick? Was it too late, and I couldn't get out? Was I wrapped around her finger? Well, I'll get right to the marriage part. December 28, 2006, we married at the Justice of the Peace in the Cumberland County Courthouse in Carlisle, Pennsylvania; and she was pregnant with our little girl. I think after that day she was not a happy bride because I didn't give her the dream wedding she had always wanted. With her first husband she had that fairy-tale wedding, and I think she wanted the same thing with me. My parents didn't not have that kind of money, and I had just returned from deployment. The last thing I was trying to do was go in debt over some wedding. I heard the horror stories about her last wedding and how it set her parents so far

61

back. I don't think to this day she will ever forgive me for not giving her that special moment in her life with her friends and her best friend. I guess that was strike one. After daughter was born on June 15, 2007, things just got worse. We stopped being a couple and a team. I guess I gained a little weight and didn't look like that super soldier she met before, that's what Post-Traumatic Stress disorder (PTSD) does to you. It changes your appearance sometimes and makes you feel left out from others. Now about this time I was starting my PTSD treatment at Walter Reed Army Medical Center as well. I was on some heavy medications for a while.

While I was home, we were at each other's neck because of the baby crying all the time and I slept all the time because of my meds. I was not a father figure to her when she was baby. During this whole time, we relocated to Harrisburg, Pennsylvania, to a much larger house than we lived in before. We were rushed into buying because we really needed a place to live with the baby and all. Interest rates were high at the time, and I didn't really care because I liked the place and we were happy. It was close to her parents. Those are words I hate to this day. I married a girl who would not move away from her family. She wasn't about to start a new life somewhere where I was trained in my skill in security. So I had to find jobs around the area that benefitted her job and not mine. So I was the one suffering with the low-income job for some time. For a while, we lived off my military retirement and my VA percentage of 90 percent. If you add all that together, that's not a lot for the whole month with our new bills and now her new bills that I'm just finding out about. Oh, I can't forget her little job. She had part–time at the hospital and some community outreach center in the city that paid nothing compared to what I was bringing in. I'm not going to list our expenses, but we had a hell of a monthly mortgage each month plus utilities. I did not have a full-time or even a part-time job yet. For a while that's the way things were going. Then I scored a few different jobs, and now I'm with the government working this DOD job. Things are slow, and my wife is working on her master's degree. She has her bachelors in whatever, and she keeps telling me that she is going to be getting a teaching job for nursing. With her current job, she has no insurance for our daughter and I don't even think she has a 401K. I am supporting everything, and I have been doing this for almost ten years now. Am I happy? *No!* Why am I staying? I am staying because she wants the best for daughter, and I agree. If she wanted to use the system in Pennsylvania, I would be a broke man. I don't really understand the system, but for ten years I've been supporting my family with my VA pension and my military retirement. I get nothing from that, and I'm always hammered on why I want money from her account, not our account. We have a joint account, and she has her own private account with another bank that I know she is putting some money back somewhere.

Have you ever gone to the store to buy a simple product and try to use your credit card and you're in line behind a bunch of people and you have PTSD? You get up to the teller to pay for your items, and your card is declined for insufficient funds. Then everyone is looking at you, and people are making comments about you. You can hear them talking about you under their voices, and your Post-Traumatic Stress Disorder kicks in, and you try to walk away. Next, you get on the phone and call your wife, and she answers the phone with, "Why are you pulling money out of the main account?" At this time I'm about to lose it on the phone with my wife asking her why I don't have any money in my account. I said, "I am a hard-working person." This is not the first I have gone to the store when my credit card was declined for financial reasons. Because of my PTSD, I let my wife budget our bills. I used to budget my bills before I was married, but I didn't have any bills. Now I'm married, and I've never seen so many bills in my life. So I left the spending and budgeting to my wife. I've talked to my doctor/counselor at the VA hospital, but it's just like a friendly conversation and he takes some notes or asks me that question: "Do you feel like you're going to hurt yourself or anyone else around you?" It's always the same questions since I've been out of WTU. I have just been going to counseling and nothing else. Nothing else recommended for me. If you ask me wife, she will tell you I'm crazy, I shouldn't be around my daughter, and I don't know how to talk to people. I just don't like being manipulated like at psychiatric patient by my wife and that's why I don't like being around her. That's why I grew away from her, and the only reason I go to my house is to see my daughter. I work hard to support them and put my daughter through private school, but when I come over to visit all I get is, "This bill's late, and we are out of money." Then she tries to tell me not to try come back into their lives or move back in. I lived with my eighty-four-year-old father in his apartment on his couch. She was going to get a lawyer and take me to the bank for everything I'm worth. I've put everything I've earned into the house they are in right now and plan to fix up that place with some new furniture and lawn furniture for the back porch. I am not going to have some home-wrecker take this away from me.

SAM007

TAKE ME AWAY FROM THIS DREAM OF THE ROSE

Once you stood so tall and bright and still as stone.
Hanging in this upright position because you are dead.
Your world is dark and gray.
Just waiting for the slightest chill to blow you away.
You're alone, because you are made this way.
There's no future for you.
For years and years, you'll hang on these walls,
until your pedals fall one by one or until I throw you away on a rainy day.
This was a dream, only a dream.
Never to come true.
Nothing is ahead because all ahead is dead.
Life is dream, until you die.

SAM007

WHY HE ALWAYS CALLS

Sitting here in this room with you, and the phone just will not stop ringing. "Who could it be this time?" A friend I'm always told by you. Always a friend. Someday, something more. Why me, always me? I am just trying my best to be myself and a good person for you. Day and night this phone just continues to ring off the hook.

Why?

This guy, but who? Just a friend, I'm always told by you.

For some reason this shit always happens to me. Why do all these guys call you? What do you do to make these guys call you? I don't even want to know. You're always telling me that this will "Stop."

Please!

It's like you think I'm dumb or something like that.

When will these calls ever stop?

Never.

You made a choice, and now you must pay.

A bill, a never-ending bill.

A call and now you're stuck with them all.

One thing is for sure is, my number isn't on your list any more.

If I were you, I would change your number and go buy a pager.

SAM007

BOXCAR SONG

Standing with my ear to the rail. Listening for the ten o'clock train to pick me up. Waiting to see my special girl. There has been some distance between us two for some time. I'm off on a journey to find her. Out there, wherever she may be, wandering along the tracks. I'm set to find her if it kills me. Sitting in this cold, damp boxcar, I travel back and forth from rail to rail to find her. All I want is for her to be with me. I may not have anything, but if I find her…I'll need nothing. This was my boxcar song.

SAM007

COWBOY ON A STRING

Kansas is an open land of nothing and no one. Here I am on my horse thinking of you. You're waiting and waiting for me. Listening to the wind, I can hear your voice calling my name. As I ride into the sunset, my shadow fades away. You will never know the truth because this is a dream. I am the wild cowboy that you caught on a string.

SAM007

ANOTHER JOKE

There was a time when people were like objects. This is how it was during the time when kings and queens ruled throughout the lands. There was one who was selected to make the royal couple laugh.

If not, "Off with their heads."

This person was different from all of us.

A person different from everyone who even tried to make them laugh.

He moved closer and closer to where the royal couple sat.

He began to speak, as their heads turned toward him.

He knew the position that he could face, if he could not make them laugh.

It's time, time for a show.

Then, the king stood up and called for his jesters one by one.

Joker was gone.

SAM007

A SIGN FROM ABOVE

Born under the zodiac sign, ruled by the moon, I am here to protect you from all. I will find out your each and every secret that you may hide. I want to seduce you, one step at a time. In the end, I want to make love to you. I am an element in your life, which you have chosen to be with.

You, the sign of the scales, ruled by Venus, the goddess of love. Ready to open yourself, ready for anything. As two, we will come together as one. On the next full moon, our juices will flow. Sharing the good and the bad and happy and the sad. All I want is you. For me to be positive and true.

I am determined to make you mine, under the zodiac sign.

SAM007

BURNING

Burning, a feeling that burns deep inside me. Burning brighter and hotter than any other flame. When I see you, I lose control of myself?

My mind is in another world.
Your world.
You control this all.
You control everything in this world.
You control me.
Building this flame between us two. Just you and me. Brighter and brighter this will get.
Let it burn. Don't blow it out. Don't pinch the wick. Let it burn all the way down.
Burning.

SAM007

THERE'LL COME A DAY

The days are getting shorter, and the nights are getting longer. There's a slight chill in this November air. I'm sitting here spot watching and waiting. All the voices have stopped. There's no more crying because all that was created has ended. The birds no longer sing; the children no longer play. The land where I once stood is now dead because of man's ability to destroy. Only a few have survived, and soon, all of them will be gone.

More and more poison is spread throughout this land. There was a day that had been written in the many books or years that he would come. The sea would be dry, and sky would turn dark. The fire would come from the underworld. There's nothing I can really say or do. Just time is all we have. This hole that I have dug with my bare hands will be my final resting spot. I am broken and can no longer go on with life this way. "I am dying!"

This is how I felt when I saw that last flash of light in the November sky on that eve of death.

SAM007

LOST SOULS

They say when you die your soul departs your body and goes to heaven or hell. It really all depends on how you died or what kind of person you really were. Some souls can't rest until they search out for what they are looking for. If you listen really close at night while on a night walk or just sitting in your bed, you just might hear these little voices or crying. These are the lost souls. Some things in their lives weren't right when they died. Now they are trying to find and fix what makes them roam the earth's floor at night. For the ones who failed, you still might hear stories about them. Wherever you may go or whatever you may do in the future, this could be you. So remember, while you're still alive, it's okay to make mistakes because in the long run they'll catch up to you. You just might become a lost soul if you're not careful in the end.

SAM007

A STYLE LOCKED AWAY

This is a kind of style that I cannot describe. As I think to myself and I wonder, *Where do these visions come from at night?* Creations in my mind and where do they come from? Thinking of the destruction and where the world stands today. We are trying our hardest to bounce back from what it used to be. Pictures in my mind, words I can't even describe. Someday!

This will all be real. For now, it's this style locked away in my mind. Just hurting and pain that the world feels. Until this all stops. The magical pictures in my mind will be a dream.

SAM007

CENTERED

Sitting in this crazy world locked behind these walls, knowing I'm safe where I stand for now. On the outside, crime is happening every minute on the hour. And I'm trying to hear through these walls. I look out the window, and it's near the crack of dawn. The ground is covered with last night's snowfall. Listening to the howl of the wind and watching the ice form on my windows. I turn back to face my room. The floors shine, and the walls enclose me in this shell around me. All alone, I am here to learn the basic principles of *leadership* and to perform a mission to the *standard*. There's a lot of stress and a lot studying. In the end, this will pay off because all will know that I am a junior NCO.

SAM007

DISTANCE

When I am with you, we have our good and bad days. Without these bad days everything would be perfect. I'm feeling this distance between you and I. What could this be this time?

Could this be the many stories I need to get off my chest and out of my mind?

From the sound of things, you feel like some object that you are not. You mean more to me than you think.

I cannot understand this distance that you want me to understand. So just close your eyes, and everything will be all right. You will not feel any more pain inside or any pain that you are feeling because of this distance.

SAM007

SLEEP

Lying in my bed, twisting and turning the night away. I finally calmed down, and my body is at the resting stage. People ask the question, why do we sleep? The body can only go so long before it breaks down. The body must rest and rebuild itself for the next day. We need power to perform. Our minds need to relax, and our muscles have to rest too. Your mind is slowing down, and your eyelids are getting heavier. All the thoughts in your mind are at a halt. The body goes through many changes when we sleep. Our blood cells are being restored, and we never notice this process is going on. The dream process is also taking place, and our minds are going through many changes. After all the energy is restored, this little alarm clock wakes you up and tells you it is time for another day. After work the body is tired and needs to start the restoring process once again.

SAM007

A DEAD FLOWER

One time you used to bloom so bright.
You stood taller than all the others.
You were filled with the many colors.
Now you are dead!
Your petals are black and you are dull.
You will never be again because of the pain that once was.
Here is your final resting stop, for you to fade deep within the earth
that once kept you from once before.

SAM007

SAD DAY

You cried, I wondered why.
I know I lied to you, to your heart and against our love.
There's nothing better than you because of me in the wrong.
I hear no more love song.
A part of me wants to stay; a part of me wants to say good-bye.
I feel there is nothing that I can say or do, to be with you.
You're going your way and I'm going my way.
Just remember, today is sad day.

SAM007

WHY WE ARE CALLED WHAT WE ARE

They call us the big green machine. Let's break it down to the basics. What are we? We are just plain everyday people who like to dress like tress and like to tell people what to do from 0500 until close of business. We change as soon as this green crash suit comes off. What does the green do for us? It hides us from others. They say, "It makes us *hard-core* and mean as *shit*."

For some of us.

We showed everyone who could stand or who could fall. All we are, we are people trained to perform, to do a mission, and carry it out with orders. We are all alike in some way or another. Brothers and sisters in the same force, fighting for the same freedom and the same rights.

We are American Soldiers.

SAM007

BUILDING CHARACTER

On this day I sit here waiting and waiting. (*Nothing*). This has to be the worse day ever to find out that she is somewhere with this other person instead of me. What a crushing day to find out some news like this. I'm a target, getting darts thrown at me every day.
Why me, always me?

All I remember was saying something about this test.
"I'm testing you."
So what did we both learn from this day? We are both feeling like total shit.

I told you time and time again.
I'm not like all your others in the past.
I'm not the kind of person to be toyed with.
Let's break it all down!

I hate this relationship test because I don't need a grade like a school student. Someone didn't trust me from the start. To have a relationship and love, you need to have confidence, honesty, and trust. Without these three parts of building character between two people, you have nothing.

I think after this day you have to realize how much we are meant to be together. You still have these blind spots that keep you from seeing your weaknesses.

So I'm glad you're feeling the way you are feeling on this day because you know it still hurts when you think about it. You deserve everything you got coming to you, all of it!

In the future events, things will be at a different point of view. So I've learned something about this building character thing is that I have to watch what I say and do because I don't want to hurt anyone. I really did care about you, but for now you are gone, and I am lost and losing my character. I just have to start over and watch others around me.

SAM007

MARCH DAY

On this eve before this March day ends, you're out there somewhere but where?

I don't know where you could be?

I don't know what you could be doing?

You don't know where I am?

Maybe, I'm lost.

Maybe not.

Your mind has given up, you've stopped.

You no longer think about when he will return. Each night I count the
  stars, thinking about the times we had together.

Have you waited or have you gone on with someone else?

I'm coming very soon.

Is there something wrong?

Do you have a lot to do and think about things between us?

Do your studies keep you up at night and you forget me

or am I just a dream in your mind?

If you don't tell me, I'll find out in the future because I will know the truth
on that March day.

SAM007

A BROKEN HEART

All of us have a heart, but some of us like to break these hearts. These people wonder why they do this kind of thing to others. There is a time in life where we reach a point that we just can't cope with this other person any longer. So we go out and meet other people. Some of us are the kind of people who just fall in love, can't give up, and will not part with that other special person in their life. The heart will always be cracked, but the mind will never forget the pain. Once the heart was full, and now it is empty. The feeling is gone. No pain, no sorrows. It's time to start all over again. The blackness is now red again. The heart is pure and full, just like before when someone came along and made you feel like you're on top of the world. Then they turn around, rip your heart out, and step all over you again and again. Then they will move on to better things in life than you. The heart will always be broken and filled with darkness because of the pain. Someone will always come along and hurt you because they enjoy this. This is the kind of person they will always be because they set out to break each and every heart they may meet.

SAM007

ART

The many different colors we see through our eyes may someday change our lives.
I gave you my soul.
This is my style.
This is my art.
For you, my love, I gave you my heart.
Like a shadow, I will cover you.
I am a part of you.
You are a part of me.
Together, we will make it through the bad, and in the end, we will both be happy.
This is my art that I will give to you forever, from the bottom of my heart.
I will close my eyes and open my mind to you because I fell in love with you.
This is my art.
You will always be a part of my art and my life.
Something, I want to take with me forever is my art.

SAM007

A COLD DAY FROM HELL

On this day, I sit here in my own world looking to the outside;
I can hear the howl of the wind making a strange sound that I'd never
heard before.
On this day, I thought to myself, *This must be the coldest day yet.*
As it started to end, I made that call. One ring and two rings.
Then I heard her voice on the phone. From the sound of her voice,
I knew this wasn't going to be a good thing between the two of us.
Something wasn't right?
Something was different?
I felt the coldness from her heart.
But why? I wondered.
Then, there was no answer, no sound.
Her voice was gone. There was nothing but a faint dial tone and silence.
This was a cold day for me. Our relationship had been crushed.
By who?
Sometimes, I still feel the coldness that she left for me.

SAM007

THE SANDMAN

Long ago, when I was a small boy I heard stories about this man who watched all the little children when they went to sleep. From what I hear, they say he walks on the air and carries a magical pouch of dust wherever he may go. He only comes out at night, just before all the little ones are in their dream state. He stopped by and sprinkled magical dust in their eyes. This would make them doze for many hours at time. You can't hear or see him while you're awake. When and if you do go to sleep, he may be your tour guide in and out of your dreams. Sometimes he will let you go in your dreams, just to see how far you may get. Just before something really terrible happens to you, he will be there to wake you from that nightmare. Then you will wake up and rub the sand from your eyes. So! Be good, little boys and girls, because if you aren't, I'll tell to him to forget to wake you from your terrible nightmares. *Dreams!* He's out there walking the nightly skies. The Sandman may just stop by and visit your house tonight.

SAM007

THE STORY BEHIND THE 29-CENT STAMP

As I write these words of wisdom to you, there is a story behind each and every line.

Night after night I sit and write.

These stories are short and true.

The stories are sometimes long, but never dull.

As I write, I wonder where this will go.

So! Am I on a long journey every night to the postbox?

Where do my magical lines go?

From post to post or coast to coast?

I will never know what has become of this.

I guess it's just a 29-cent stamp, lick and drop into an empty box.

SAM007

COVERED

There you are to be noticed by all. You're in your own world, and people just do not understand your actions. You are going step-by-step because of past relationships you wish not to remember. There must be something about you.

Is it:

Personality?

Style?

Body?

Creativity?

Maturity?

Interest?

Sense of humor?

Clothing?

Music?

Or is it the Inner you or all of the above. No one can change you or the way you are. You are you, and I like you for the way you are.

SAM007

STRANGE WAYS

At one time, she was just an object to me. I then went my own way, not worrying about anything that lay ahead of me. Now I sit in this chair thinking about how she feels. There is something I have to tell her. I don't really want to hurt her feelings. I just want her to understand the truth. "You are the only one I ever wanted, until now." All you like to do is go out with others and do things I don't even want to say. This isn't over yet because I'm watching and waiting for you to make your each and every move. Then I will catch you, red-handed. Then you will know the truth about everything within my soul, everything I have been hiding from you. So do what you want to do. Your day is coming. I will end your little games sooner or later. You broke my heart. I'm watching you. Soon you will slip. Then you will sit here just like me with nothing. Boy! You sure are something strange, but I'm really glad this ended before it started.

SAM007

THANKSGIVING CRY

Thanksgiving is the time for giving thanks for all. On this day I have nothing to be thankful for except for this big empty space. I had everything, and I lost it. She's there, and I'm here. Sitting here, waiting for time to go by. Nothing I can say or do because it is all up to you. You're waiting for this magical change to happen. The change is really between the two of us and no one else. Why do I do all these things to you? I know you could care less what I may do. Years and years and I'm with someone like you. This really started to build and go somewhere, but where? Maybe someday, if this is true and next year I'm with you. For now we remain apart. I really did love you and hoped on this day of thanks, you would stop and think for a second about what you're missing. Remember the times together and, most of all, my cries of thanks.

SAM007

IN THE MASTER'S EYE

On this night, I am ill. I walk to the window to take a look. I look out the window to notice the ground is covered with last night's fresh snowfall. I'm watching the snow build its own winter wonderland. I began to think of you. Each and every snowflake is different from the other. There are big one and small ones. There are all shapes and all sizes, but there is only one in the Master's Eye. So perfect in style and form. So perfect in grace with all the right moves. This one represents you. I will catch you in my hand so tight and make you mine, all of the time. Soon you will melt away, and you will be nothing to my eye.

SAM007

LOST

Here I am floating up in the sky so high.
I'm like a balloon without a string.
I'm floating because of you.
Higher and higher I will go.
Soon!
I will get so high, that I might just *pop*!
Then, I'll be no-longer.
Up in the sky I'm looking down at you.
You're lost because now you have nothing left.
You just let it fly away.
Let us be as one, not as two.
I only want to be with you.
For now I have no string because I am lost without you.
Fly away.

SAM007

THE CAT (NINE LIVES)

There you are all alone waiting to make your perfect move in the darkness, hidden in a corner. I can see your sexy bright eyes. I am smelling you, waiting for you, and wondering what you taste like. I want to explore all the parts of your body and wondering where I start. Moving undetected, you notice a strange figure a few feet away. Your body begins to tingle, and you are feeling warm all over yourself. Your mind is telling you one thing, and your heart is telling you something else. Then there is a brief connection between the two of us. Then it's quiet, and she is gone. Slick as a Cat she has disappeared. Nine lives following your every path, wherever you may go. Alone you are waiting for her.

There is still some type of communication between you two, but soon it will be lost. Trying for months, you try to come up with a plan that will not fail. Never wanting to break away, but you must because of the many barriers that stand between you two. It has been building slowly, and you have been trying to find out what makes her purr. Knowing someday the Cat and you would be together. After that, what will this become?

Distance! A space that is between two people wanting to have each other, but there are gaps stopping the dream process. You both are having visions of each other and getting wetter as you think about it. We are both empty because of others and their problems that delay this action from happening. The Cat is out with her hat, wearing her smile and lusting, feeling to open herself to you. Again, the Cat has gone into the sea of darkness, waiting for the perfect move, if she ever can.

SAM007

MUSIC

Music was created to please the mind, the body, and the soul. Music is a part of our everyday life. We listen to it while we are awake or asleep; it makes us feel relaxed. It makes us want to dance or jump around in to a crowd at a concert.

Music comes in many different forms, starting out with someone hitting two stones together in the early days to create a sound or what we call a beat. To this day, we use computers to edit and mix beats. Music will always exist because someone is always making a new beat or dubs. We hear music in the streets, at the office, in the schools, at home, or in the dance clubs.

I'm a person who cannot live without music. It takes the stress away and brightness the day. If it is not a CD or a digital download, I'm always playing with it. Listening to the beat or following the words, and I use my fingertips to sample this sound. I am always trying to create a new beat or sound.

Music is like sex. You can't ever get enough, and there is something better out there every month. You just have to look and see what your taste is in these sounds. Good for him and good for her. The never-ending sound, which we call a beat. Music will never die.

SAM007

A FARAWAY DREAM

There is girl that I've known for a very long time. It was time to depart from the relationship and say "Good-bye." We both went different directions in life. One thing we never did was lose contact between each other. Then one day Uncle Sam took me off to War to be with him. I thought I would be lost at this time. I haven't heard from her in months. Then one day something came for me in the mail. I knew she wouldn't give up on me, but something happened! Now she's going through the same thing I went through for months and months. Now she knows how I felt at this time of my life. There's more to the story. What kind of relationship did we go through?

One time we were friends, and the next we were at each other necks. There sure is a lot to think about here. Is this really worth saving? She's out there somewhere, but where? Are you this far away dream I may never see or hear from again? I know one thing! You'll always be that faraway dream I will never forget. The War has ended, and I have returned to nothing. The dream of you will never go away, and all that remains is a secret that you had left on my bed before you left me that last time.

SAM007

LOOKING

Here in this open range, I feel the winter wind blowing from north to south. I can feel the winter chill moving throughout and about. The sky is gray, and there is not a cloud in sight. I have a long wait before I rest for the night. Just time is all I have. There is nothing across this open land, and I don't knowing what lies ahead of me. I must stay alert at all times, or I'll die. I am looking for a sign, for anything. The hours pass and so do the seconds. I've reached the point I have been looking for. Soon tomorrow will come, and I will set off once again. For now the land is still, and the stars are far away at night. The last part of night fades away from sight. I just close my eyes and say *"Good night."*

SAM007

NO FREEDOM

Sitting in this world of hate and crime, someone is dying every second and every hour. I write this while others are being born in hospitals. Here I sit so high in the sky watching your each and every move. And people are doing whatever they what to do of their own free will. This is known as "Freedom." At one time, we used to be like stock or trade. Then a bill was passed for the Freedom of Speech, Freedom for our Rights, and Freedom of the Press. I can say whatever I want to say to you, and you can say whatever you want to say to me. Today as the world stands, we are running wild. Everyone is trying to run the government, but only one can run that seat. The world is hurting, and we are hurting ourselves. In the end, our freedom may have gone too far. Our freedom caused this world to be where it is today. Our freedom could cause us to destroy each other someday. I say, "Take heed because man's freedom will only go so far." Soon man will end what man has created. Do we really have the right to do whatever we want?

SAM007

MORNING

Here in my trench, I watch a new day takes its toll. Waiting and waiting for any kind of movement along the horizon. Knowing the position at where I sit could be hit at any time. Looking into the small town that crests over the hill. Watching each and every light go out as the sun breaks through the clouds.

Good morning and knowing it could turn into a bad day at any time because of the force that lies ahead of me. Hidden, so I can't see them. Without any fear, I just sit here because I am ready to die. Knowing she is somewhere waiting for my safe return. That's the fire burning within our hearts that makes me survive.

SAM007

FIRE IN THE EYE

A candle burns in the dark room as you sit at a desk looking into a never-ending flame. Your eyes are locked on a target, and only you can put out this flame. Looking deep into this flame, where only the colors make up this flame. Fire is the start of life. Fire tells a story.

The *blue* represents how free you are.

The *white* represents how pure your heart is. There is a blank spot is your mind for a few seconds, and now you see *red*.

The *red* represents how your life feels, but now it's all a *big* nothing and hollow sound, just like the room you sit in is empty.

The *orange* represents the truth of life.

This is the fire in your eye. Only you can control this flame. You're now waiting for the perfect moment to end all this. Now there a silence; your eyes are closed. The fire is out, and the room is cold. A flame that only you controlled is now gone because you just let it go and didn't care what happened. The flame got lower and lower, and it has burned out. *Nothing*!

SAM007

THAT KIND OF LOOK

She's standing there with the power in her hands. She starts to move out of the corner of the room. I sit here in this chair in this room. I can see her as the sun hits the front of her face. I noticed how clear she looks to me. I watched her movement at the door. I said to her, "Your eyes tell a story, but I don't understand you. Your feelings are strong, and your hunger is there." She says, "You'll just never understand my feeling for you."

As the sight of her fades away, I watch the last light from the crack of the door as it closes behind her. I noticed the door stayed ajar for a minute as I went to take a look. All I could remember was that special kind of look that she gave me. This must have been some kind of hint because she was behind the door with this magical stare. The interest is there, but how can I get it from her?

Now she is gone forever. Remember, that kind of look must have meant something, and someday I'll know that she really was trying to say something to me as she said, "*Good-bye.*"

SAM007

THREE SIGNS OF A CLOVER

Walking down the narrow path in the forest, you stumble upon a wicked bridge. As you start to cross, you hear a voice from the bridge. You look around to see where the voice came from. You notice in the darkness from under the bridge an evil short troll. He lets no one pass without the special password. You hold the key to life and to success. On the other side of the bridge death awaits you and so do the troubles that you worry about in your mind daily. The troll pulls out this special solid, clear object. He holds your future in the palm of his hand. Remember as you look into the charm of evil, think about the heart. It's pure in many ways. Evil is not. Evil will try to trick you as much as it can. Faith is all you have.

Soon your body has slowed down, and the troll is watching each and every move. The troll then pulls out three magical dice from a small black silk bag. Only your chances lie with the dots on the dice. The 666 sign is the sign of Evil. Only the troll can roll this number. As the troll goes away for a second, you switch the dice. The dice you replace with the old one is now pure, like your heart and the sun that once shined before the world that you live in now. As the moon starts to peak over the mountains, a three is rolled and a six and a set of snake eyes appear. Everything is quiet, and the ground begins to shake. The troll looks puzzled as he knew his time was near the end. Evil can only go so far.

In the end, the troll had lost. No more guards on the wicked old bridge anymore. Sometimes there is a blank in the mind that only you can solve. No one else controls it. Luck is all you have to live with. Too much luck can run out. There are four leaves on a clover. The luck that many hear about is within the fourth leaf. Once that leaf is picked off from the other three, there is no longer any luck remaining. So keep all the leaves together when you find theses clovers. Fairy tales can go forever, but stories will always end in some way or another at that old wicked bridge.

SAM007

PICTURES OF YOU

Here I sit looking at these pictures of you, remembering our good and our bad days. Each and every individual picture tells a story that I'll never forget nor will I ever look away from. It brings the brightness out in you. Away from this picture, I can see and feel you. I feel like you're right here beside me, feeling me, making love to me, keeping me on the right path, and keeping me warm. It's like 3D. I can step right into the picture with you and disappear to a far-off place. I can disappear to the Land of Oz or the land of no return. Then I open my eyes, and you're right there standing and looking me dead in the face. Is it me? Or am I in this magical, colorful, faraway place and wondering what to do next?

SAM007

FAR FROM HOME

Here in Korea I sit all alone, feeling like day 365 will never come. "In time," I'm told. It's getting colder and colder, and stress is following us everywhere we go. Our time clocks ticks on, and death is right at my side. We are missing our families and our loved ones. Today, I sit here writing to my special gift that *God* himself has said, "*Yes*, you both are meant to be." So far from home I think about you. Looking for your open arms and waiting to rub myself against your warm body. I see visions of you in the mirror. When I open my eyes, I'm in a room with four walls looking right back at me. Knowing in this room where I sit, there is a story to tell from each and every soldier who has stayed here before me. Thinking of the motherland, I am thinking about the job I must do because of what we represent and when we are needed. Stuck in this land where everything is backward. I am a long way from home, and soon this will all end.

SAM007

BETWEEN SOMETHING
AND NOTHING

Why am I the way I am? Why do I do the things I do to you? Why do
   you enjoy these things? I'm sorry I hurt you, but I never really noticed
   that I did this to you.
Your secrets should only be between you and me. Not the entire world.
At times, I thought there was something but really it was nothing.
I'm not sure why I do this. I guess it's all a part of me.
Nobody else to touch you but me and only me, for my pleasure.
My special friend, my lover. That could have been you.
Why not me?
Trying to build something that never would have lasted.
What was it Love or Hate?
Maybe some just big freaking game.
There was something?
But now it's *nothing*!

SAM007

THE PASSING OF TIME

Time is passing and passing, the days are going by. You're there in the high lands and I'm here in the low lands. Driving night and day, stopping for nothing and no one. The rain is about to set in, and the clouds are low. Soon! The fog sets along the horizon. There's nothing out there I can see any more on this night. Now I must stop. Not knowing what could pop out of this nightly wall of darkness. I am lost and missing something I need. It's not the same without you anymore. Soon, I'll be on my way back up to you, at least in the end. I'll be sure because we will be together as one, not as two. The forces collided together, trying to end what we have together. I will end my search until I reach out and find what I looking for, if I have to live or die trying.

SAM007

FEAR OF THE NIGHT

As the day comes to an end, I look out at the mountains. They appear to form a wall around me. I am watching and waiting for the first light to appear in this dark sky, listening to the sounds of the night. As time got longer into the night, I could feel the slightest chill in the air. I was waiting for the slightest movement around me. Something is out there, but I don't know what it could be? Always waiting for what man fears the most. That eternal darkness is forever lurking, at a time when the world is dark and empty. It is like a black hole, waiting to swallow you up at any time. Nothing is on my mind, but the fear of death that awaits me. The night fades away into a cloud of gray.

SAM007

IN THE CENTER OF EVERYTHING

Standing here alone, I can see you watching me. Looking into your eyes, I can see more than just a relationship. Knowing on the other side there is this barrier, and that something will come between you and me. In this mixed-up world of adulthood, where I have pulled you into is more than just a game. The cat must play because of this force, a force that she will never feel again.

So on this night, their souls come together, twisting and turning the night away. The scent of love is in the air. They both know that somewhere something is wrong. Somewhere this must stop. But where? Who knows? This must have been some wild and crazy dream I had while I was asleep or there was more to find out about this tale? I'm left with this question? Seeing you makes me burn more and more. I am lost in this world of nothing, and I have nothing to turn to. This feeling goes deep in my heart. Sometimes it's like a double beat or thump or a pop, or it just might *stop* all together.

It is so hard to find someone so perfect and so soft. We have found each other, but this must stop. In the end, there is pain that we all must feel. We want it, but we just can't have it. I just wish I had the key to the magical door, so I could open it up and tear your soul apart to make you feel the pain that I went through for the many years. It was all a dream, but I want this to come true because I want you to understand and feel my pain you put me through.

SAM007

COMING FORCE

I stood along this road watching the last of the day fade away. I think back, *This was a good day*. The sun meets the mountains like it always does in the evening. The night thickens, the last of the night fades away, and the moon starts to take form. I'm on this road traveling closer and closer to you. Nothing will stop me from seeing you because of this force that's pulling us both together. This is your night; it's been a bad one for me. Just pull this out, and I assure you that you will feel much better because I thought of you on this night as I wrote this to you. As the forces come from every direction...every sight and every sound.

SAM007

CLOUDS

The clouds up in the sky are so high. They are moving as slow as they can across the sky. Every cloud is so different, in every shape and every size, looking like giant marshmallow piles so high in the sky. One minute the mountains are there, and the next minute they're gone. A storm is coming because I can feel it in the air. Looking into the distance, I can see the darkness moving among us. Knowing at any time it could reach this very spot. There is nowhere to run and nowhere to hide. The day will be better when the terrible storm passes by.

SAM007

THE BOY IN THE BUBBLE

Born into this world with a problem, now to remain here in my own world where the air is pure. On the outside the air is thin and dirty, where I might just die. So I'm locked up in this bubble forever. I can't feel the outside. I can only see her standing there day after day looking into my world, knowing the thoughts that are going through her mind as she stands there and stares into my eyes. I just want to reach out and feel her. Every day she visits me and sits by the bubble and talks to me for many hours, never knowing what a woman's real touch will feel like. This bubble holds me back from the rest of the open world. Someday this bubble will be gone when I wake up from this terrible nightmare. For now I wake up to feel the air circling around me, and someday I want my wish to come true, so I can play with others and touch your soft, smooth body. My world holds me back from all of that fun. The nights are quiet, and everything is still as stone. Trapped! Being the boy in the bubble, I know there is no escape from the glass cell that holds me in forever, and we will never know what is it is like to touch, taste, or smell each other.

SAM007

114

CANNON FIRE

Cannon fire is what we provide.
Cannon fire is what we do.
If there wasn't Cannon fire we would die.
With Cannon fire, we will take the pass.
With Cannon fire, we will take the hill.
With Cannon fire, we will kill.
In the end when the smoke clears, you see why we need Cannon fire.
In the end we did our jobs because we will still have Liberty and Freedom
of our rights.
Cannon fire is what we strive for.
With Cannon fire we will survive.
Cannon fire is our job.
Cannon fire.

SAM007

CHRISTMAS IN OZ

Here on this eve of Christmas, listening to holiday music. Trying to pick out the best one from when I was a kid and knowing Santa was coming on this night. I am a little older now and on my own. Wondering why it is this way. Deployments keep me away. Keep me away from you. Sitting here drinking my last glass of eggnog and watching the Christmas lights flicker on and off out on the porch. Thinking about what the future has in store for me. Empty spaces I need to fill because I am sick of being alone on nights like these. Like a game of chess that I am always playing, waiting for the perfect move. *No* snowflakes in Kansas. *No* snow in "Oz." I sit here as I watch the clock hit twelve o'clock. Knowing one thing and that is I am home for Christmas in the Land of Oz.

SAM007

STOCKING STUFFER

On this eve of Christmas, I sit in this room all alone, drinking my soul away from this bottle. The sounds of Christmas music playing are heard in the background. I guess you're wondering why I'm here at night like this. She thought our relationship was too much. What a night to tell someone news like this. Boy! I really got my stocking stuffer this year! Now I sit here and think, *Why did I ever waste my time with someone like this?* Right now I could be with family or friends or loved ones who really care about people or maybe you? So I am crushed on this Eve of Christmas.

Tomorrow is Christmas, and to me the gift is gone. It feels like just another day of the year. I'm here alone in my room, all cooped up in this corner. It feels like these walls a closing in on me. As Christmas nears, I hope she feels the same way I am feeling as I write this short but true story. I am twisting and turning the night away. I thought I could be beside her on this night, holding her close and tight and keeping her warm by the fire. She thought this would be too much. Now she's gone!

Someone just took Christmas away from me this year. Last year at this time I was off to war and thinking that I wasn't coming back. "So, Santa Claus, if you are real and you can hear me, please bring me something special or something to brighten my day." What Merry Christmas and ho-ho-ho stocking stuffer I got this year! So, dear *Lord* who died on the cross and who was born on this day, that is what Christmas is all about. That's what it means to me. What about a tree or gift? My gift is to be alive and free. Santa, sorry no stocking stuffers this year.

(Written on December 24, 1991)

SAM007

A PERSON IS ONLY A SHELL FROM THE OUTSIDE

As I walk around, people look at me. They can only see me by my outer shell and the way I dance. Some of them know me better than others. When you see me most of the time, I'm usually alone. I am never with a woman, just by myself because of the many problems in the past. Sometimes I am with the boys, enjoying a beer or maybe two. Three is pushing the limit, and four is the max. My body tells me when to stop, so I don't get myself in trouble. When people evaluated me, they said I am sharp and still as stone. I do whatever I want to do. I set out to do what I need to do, and I get it done. I move on to newer and better things in life. I never smile because I am always concentrating on the mood and the sounds around me. It seems like I'm dead from inside. But really, if you get to know me, you'll get to understand me a lot better. There really is a true and bright person inside this shell of darkness. I am always on my own because that is the way it always has been.

There is no one to tell me *shit*! I guess you could say my characteristics are different from others. I do it, and that's it. So remember! When you look at someone, don't judge them by the way they look. They might not seem to be the person you really think they are. They just might end up hurting you.

Don't judge a book by its cover.

SAM007

TWENTIETH-YEAR CLASS REUNION SPEECH

I stand here tonight as a highly decorated noncommissioned officer/soldier to tell you that if I had to do it again, would I?

However, after my many tours of duty with over twenty years of military service, I must admit that I am ready to retire.

Since graduation, I have kept in touch with a few classmates or bumped into you here or there. I think after high school I grew closer to a certain group of people from these social media groups sitting in this room tonight. A lot of you have moved on with your lives elsewhere, but like the famous movie line in *The Wizard of Oz*, "There's no place like home." Carlisle is our home and where our roots are.

Class, as we sit here tonight, I would like you to think back and remember how you were treated or how you treated others.

Tonight, we are here to relax, network, and enjoy a long-lasting fellowship. Some of you may know what it is like to be in my shoes. Tonight, as we sit here, please take a moment to think about our loves ones who are currently serving and are deployed overseas and remember those who have lost their lives as a result of this terrible war.

I would like to thank my wife and my one-year-old daughter. Thank you for everything and your love. Becoming a father has been the best thing that has happened to me in my life. It has changed my priorities and my goals in life.

In closing, let's not forget those many different groups that separated us in high school and try to embrace each and everyone in this room tonight. I am thankful to have the opportunity to share in this evening's activities with you all.

SAM007

96 HOURS

I am not sure if I know how to describe this as I lay in my bed thinking about how this is all going to come out on paper. On December 26, 1990, I was nineteen years old heading to Kuwait on an aircraft with the soldiers of Bravo (Bulls) Battery 2-1 Field Artillery and the rest of the First Armored Division. I was thinking, *What did I sign up for, and am I really going to war so soon?* It was as though Christmas had come and gone, the spirit was gone so quick that we didn't even have time to open any gifts this year.

Next thing I knew, we were in Kuwait or somewhere in the Middle East, but they would not tell us where. All I know is that when I stepped off that plane, it was as though the life was sucked out me because I had never been in any situation like this before. There was no airport, just a lot of blowing hot ass sand, and it was really *hot*. I don't even think we had time to acclimate. We inventoried everything we had and headed right to the port to pick up our equipment.

I think we spent four days at the port unloading everything, putting it on trucks, and when we got to a certain location, that was it. It was as if we were on our own, and everyone went a different direction. Things are not very clear to me because this was twenty-five years ago. Yet I remember we used the phonetic alphabet to move from location to location. I was just a young private who was told to dig fighting positions and a power pits to throw our extra powder increments away when we were done firing our missions. My job during Desert Shield preparation was to run powder increments to foxholes about fifty yards away from the howitzer fighting position. When I wasn't doing anything, I sat on the howitzer, rear left spade, and watched the crew drill. This was our life. If you were not part of the gun crew, you remained outside preparing ammunition with the Ammunition Team Chief. Most of time I was digging survival pits.

We spent a lot of time in the desert firing missions to nowhere, but we soon learned that we were no longer in rear to direct support. We were going to be firing from the frontlines with tanks directly at the Iraqi Republican Guard. All I know is that day turned into night because of the burning oil fields and life was not getting any better the further we progressed toward the border.

It was as if we had no artillery training skills except for the ones from Basic and AIT. I think we learned more skill to survive in the desert heat than anything. For a while, we were the only ones in desert. We didn't see any other units or tanks or infantry soldiers. It was almost as if they were all behind us, and we were out in front by ourselves on a suicide mission or something. We starting eating MREs three times a day, and the mail stopped coming to the soldiers who received mail. It was as though we were cut off from the rest of the Division.

We were given instruction to move in the dark without night vision, and when we got there, we dug in and did not move until after ninety-six hours. There were a lot of sand dunes around us, and it was very hard to see the other howitzers. We used the terrain to cover ourselves, and we dug in as our lives depended on it. As we sat, we were addressed over the speaker system in our howitzers by our commander telling us how good of a battery we were and that he wanted every soldiers to come back after what we were about to diminish ahead of us. Due to the minimal training that we had as a battery, he trusted in *God* for our survival because we were the frontline. And when the war started and the shit hit the fan, we stayed in place to provide indirect fire support for the entire 1 AD and units crossing the border of seventh Corps.

I will tell you now; it was as if the Republican Guard knew where we were. As soon as we heard a crack in the sky, meaning incoming artillery, we had mission after mission. I did my job as a private. I ran in the trench we dug, the hole way back to the powder pit, and dropped my increments as many as I could. We were nonstop, but we kept taking incoming artillery and provided fire for whoever needed it. It was as though we were meant to die as a battery in place. I never saw so many great soldiers and NCOs in a split second when a T72 tank came into our position and was hunting us like sheep. Everyone went to ground, and the crews conducted direct fire operations on that single tank. I won't say it was a confirmed kill, or KIA, but that tank did not come back. I think M1 got him later during the war. That day I saw my life flash in front of my eyes, and then we got the call that the president (POTUS) was about to come on national TV in the states to declare a *cease-fire*. Well, we did not get the word. I was listening to my chief say, "We are going to do one last stand and completely destroy the IRG until they were no more."

At that moment something happened inside the howitzer. It was as though someone had ripped the number 1 man cannoneer's hand off. He had broken his wrist on the breech and could not fire the forty-five-round fire mission at the end of the war. With no artillery training, but just what I learned in basic and watching while I was assigned to the section, I was up. My chief had no other option but to put me inside the howitzer to fire the mission as we sat in place to receive any enemy direct or indirect fire during that mission.

Fire mission! Forty-five rounds! SHELL, HE, FUZE PD, CHRG 8 Red Bag. That's all I knew for forty-five minutes as I loaded the cannon nonstop. The howitzer crew just watched in amazement as we provided artillery fire to destroy the Iraqi Republican Guard. Now I am not going to say that it was a breeze because it took a lot out of me, and I had to crawl on top of the howitzer for a few minutes to relax because my body was broken in half. As I took just a few seconds in the dark, I looked up and noticed MLRS rockets coming from the rear of the battlefield. I felt so proud to be an American because someone was about to have a bad day. All I could see was the rocket fire from each rocket shot at the enemy.

For actions in combat during Operation Desert Shield, Operation Desert Storm, and Operation Provide Comfort as a Private First Class and my first Army award, I received an *Army Commendation Medal* for my action during the ninety-six-hour combat Operations and sitting in place of a fellow soldier to complete the mission without injury.

All together for these *operations*, every soldier who put their life on the line or gave the ultimate sacrifice earned more than respect while deployed to the Middle East/Kuwait/Saudi Arabia. The Second Battalion, First Field Artillery (no longer in existence/active) received the Valorous Unit Award, National Defense Service Medal, and Southwest Asia Service Medal with three bronze Service Campaign Stars, Kuwaiti Liberation Medal, and Saudi Arabia Kuwait Liberation Medal. Sounds like a lot, but today we are still suffering from this war known as Desert Storm Syndrome by some, but today it is known as Post-Traumatic Stress Disorder.

SAM007

SECRET BOX

There were times I used to write on pieces of paper, ball them up, and put them in my pocket for another day or keep the thoughts in my mind for when I ready to release them to the world. Messages held inside, like a genie in a bottle. Words or a sentence that hardly made sense to anyone but me. Standing lonely at night, waiting for the perfect time to write when I knew the time was right. A silence of the night blowing across my face as I could feel the sand beating my face as I wrote these short but sad and true blues of life.

Reaching into the darkness, always wanting to see if something was there to take me away, but nothing ever did. I knew my life was going nowhere because I was stuck in this box. Collecting my thoughts on paper, I had to find a place to hide all this anger but where? Complete blackness, so no one could find this until I was ready to open this box to the world. Always writing night after night and day after day until my mind was wasted.

Still I write, collecting a list of visions in my mind of everything that has happened from the start of mankind to the end of war. More pictures are created as I draw with my mind, hiding each and every incident that happened to me in sight and sound.

Going back to the pieces of paper, I balled up in my pocket. It's time to tell my story to the rest of the world, the hurting, the pain, and suffering that has been balled up for years and years. Digging deep down in to this secret box, I can feel the many pages I have stored for years and years as they began to wither between my fingers. I try to pull them out of the box.

What has become of my messages I created years ago that I have hidden from the lights of the world and sight of man himself. Now the only thing left is the mystery and empty box.

SAM007

A SPECIAL ROCK

For years and years, you have seen the face of death in the hot, dry, and cold empty Saudi Arabian desert. You lie dormant as you hear the many stories of soldiers and travelers that pass you by day after day and night after night. You've conquered and survived some of the worst sandstorms that man has ever seen or felt created by God himself. Somehow you've made it from place to place undetected. You're graceful in all you do. Your shell is like a knight's armor. You are smooth in all your moves. Created from the heavens and the earth, you're here to serve a purpose. All these stories you have locked inside you just waiting and waiting for that perfect time to share them.

One day I was out in the Middle Eastern desert walking around, kicking the sand, and being bored because I never knew when I was going home. It was my first time in combat, and I was hardly trained to do my job. I was only nineteen years old and wondering if I was going to live or die in this hellhole of a place. I looked down and found you.

For a minute I just looked at you because you were not just your everyday rock or something found in the desert. You were separated from all the others, and I knew this was something that I needed. That something was to pick you up and make mine for the rest of my life. I did not know how this was going to be, but I had to make this work. You were small enough to fit on the palm of my hand and go in my pocket when needed. You became like a guardian to me and you're not *God*, but you're like a safe keeper in my travels for me. Since then you have gone from multiple deployments, and you have heard my stories about life and death. You've seen combat operation after combat operation and stuck with me when

I needed you when I was feeling blue. I was even told that you weren't allowed to leave the Kuwaiti desert at a certain time, but you are still with me as my keeper. Today you ride with me wherever I may travel from north to south and east to west.

As I sit here and look at you, I say thank you for all the good and the bad. I never held on to something so important to me, so close to my heart, for so many years as I have done with you. Some people might think this is joke, but you're not my little toy soldier or my blanket that I cuddle with at night because you're more important than that. I might not have been born with you, but I can say you've been back and forth to hell and back with me. I will always have a special place in my heart for this rock even though you are a materialistic object. The forces of nature know where you came from and what you truly stand for, and I truly know what you stand for because you're my rock.

SAM007

WHAT IS THE CURE TO
THE PROBLEM?

As we enter into a world of darkness, pain, sorrow, and disease, where is the cure to our never-ending problems we face every day? I'm stuck in a combat zone with nowhere to go. Bullets are flying everywhere; and your fellow soldiers, friends, and comrades are dying all around you. You can't do anything but fire back at the enemy, knowing the next bullet might have your name on it. Then there's a silence in the air. You look around to see all the bodies, and your mind is going completely bonkers. No medic for miles and it's just you left all alone with everything dead and red.

Many years later you sit on the couch having just recently gotten out of the VA Hospital after horrible nightmares and visions of what you saw on the battlefield years before. Suffering from one of our number one killers of culture shock, battle fatigue, or today as we call it Post-Traumatic Stress Disorder (PTSD). Science and medical research tells us there are ways we can heal the demons or cope with our inner problems that we deal with every day. I think if you have been through a traumatic event and it digs in enough, there's no going back to reality. You're telling me, for example, the bullets you witnessed fly by your face, when you saw your life flash in front of your eyes several times, while you stood there and time stood still, you're just going to forget about this after a bunch of medical therapy and a bunch of medication that they want you to take to forget your problems and move on to the next problem?

I think there are many cures to our demons, but sometimes we have to just face them one-on-one to understand this is the only way that the demon is going to uncover itself. There will always be a black hole within us, and there is nothing we can ever do to get rid of that pain and suffering of a lost one or traumatic event in your life.

Life does not stop on the couch. Some make the choice to remain on the couch and spend their days trying to find the answers within their minds as they daydream all day long. The answer is not on the couch. The answer is reaching out and trying to find help with people and friends around you—loved ones, and family members, or just a close someone. I have seen where the VA has a person so drugged up with medication that it's the only answer in their world, but sometimes even the doctors are wrong in some cases. Medication is distributed in vast quantities to so many veterans that just about anyone can get their hands on some kind of psychiatric drug these days. Now they are introducing medical marijuana into the system, and do you really think this is going to help a PTSD patient? You're a veteran who has never smoked or drank alcoholic beverages and now you're giving them marijuana to smoke every day instead of taking pills? That's a bad call on the part of the system. Most of the time they would be high and could not operate a motor vehicle or work at a job using the system.

Again in my case, the reason why I'm writing this is because for the last three years I have been taking pain medication on top of my PTSD medication, making me high. I want to not feel pain, and I want something to stop the pain, so why not take something to never to have pain. Well, the VA recommended I take a certain type of medication for many years, and it started catching up to me. I noticed blood in my stool, and I told the VA about it. I guess you could say it was under supervision for a while because this was an off thing. I had a colonoscopy planned in the future. Well, days turn into weeks, and weeks turn into months, and the medications took their toll, and I started to bleed out. I went to the emergency room, and the doctors at the hospital told me, "My kidneys were failing and the medication I was taking for pain was not helping them." So I was admitted into the hospital for a few days, and tests were run on me. I found out that this medication I've taken for three years for pain and my PTSD has not been helping me. My body was reacting to it, and I was not noticing it until it was too late.

What is the cure for being healthy this day? Really nothing because I think eventually everything you put in your body will hurt you. I'm not saying go run out and grab a bag of medical marijuana and smoke it up. There are a lot of people out there with PTSD who should have higher ratings and they don't have the support from their local VAs. I hope you are not one of those guys or gals sitting on the couch reading this, because if you are, it's time to change your life and open up the door. It's time to find a cure to this terrible disease that has put you in a trap and holding you and your family down for years. Hey, I don't write to get my thrills out of this or to make a buck or two. I suffer from the same shit you suffer from and stood on the same battlefield you did my friend. If I can do this and come from punching walls and not talking to people to having a beautiful baby girl and being an author of a book, you can get off that couch you've been sitting on for years because we can beat this, you and I.

SAM007

STAR WARS: SOMETHING YOU DIDN'T KNOW (THE SIGNS) PTSD

Following social media, the new movie *Star Wars - Episode VII* has revealed hidden signs that we are just now uncovering. It is recommended that you read up on Ben Solo's (Kylo Ren's) childhood to understand how he was brought to the dark side by the evil emperor Snoke. Even though Kylo Ren is fantasy/science fiction, we tend to believe these characters can be real at times. So let me begin to explain what I found out from my reading.

Ben Solo never knew how he acquired the disease Post-Traumatic Stress Disorder (PTSD), but as a child he was suffering from the illness. The evil emperor watched him grow and observed his desire to be a Jedi. In his upbringing, he was forced to go to the dark side. It is said that Luke Skywalker trained Ben to fight as a Jedi, and I can't wait to see that battle when it occurs in a future episode when these two masters meet. If you take notice in the *Force Awakens*, Kylo Ren uses his three-sided light saber to destroy the computer system in the Death Star headquarters control room. I think he has a little PTSD because he goes a little crazy in the movie.

I sometimes see myself as this character Kylo Ren because sometimes there are things that set me off. I am not out of control like he appears to be because I have medication that controls my emotions and anger. Here is a guy who idolizes Darth Vader, someone who is willing to kill his own father for the dark side, so we know he really has some problems. As individuals, we all go through a time in our life where we go to the dark side. Sometimes we cannot cope with our emotions. We have to convert completely over or we are brought back to the force. However, with counseling and special therapeutic help, we are able to come back but we are never the same after a traumatic event in of life.

I highly recommend all of you review the new Star Wars movie and all the cool trailers that people are putting out on the new movie. It just makes you wonder who is returning, who the new villains will be that will help Kylo Ren, and what other characters may be coming to the dark side. If you watch all the movies from beginning to end, you will see political and governmental signs throughout the movies. As I suffer with my Post-Traumatic Stress Disorder and try to help others with worse cases, I just want to share a few of my own opinions. I want to share some things I have read about the next few movies and the latest on character updates. My thoughts might help you understand that just because these characters are fiction doesn't mean the person that the writer is trying to portray doesn't have a message to others that are watching.

"May the force be with you" and with your health and safety through the time spent with your families as you continue to read the stories and poems in these pages. I have found beyond these pages that I have written about the Republic, and I hope you continue to dream and support your favorite characters. I just thought it would be nice to add a little Stars Wars action to my book for you.

SAM007

LOCKED IN A MUSEUM OF TIME AND BEYOND

When you are a hard charger like me, what kind of hell lands you working in a military museum at the peak of your military career? Well let's rewind a few weeks back while I was still a Gunnery Sergeant in Charlie Battery First Battalion, Thirty-Seventh Field Artillery, Third BDE, 2 ID Fort Lewis, Washington. What a great location and great base to be stationed at near Mount Rainer and Seattle, Washington! There is no other place like the home of all the rock 'n' roll bands and great mountaintops on the West Coast.

For me, I guess you could say I was sitting on a time bomb in my unit because my days were numbered. It was as though someone was out to get me or liked trying to make me reach my boiling point. I guess others knew I had anger issues, but I kind of kept them to myself. There were some who tried my patience, like one of the Platoon Sergeants, who always had his way with others. I really don't know how this guy made it through the ranks to become a senior Non-Commissioned Officer or NCO. There was just something about this guy that people didn't like, and I guess he made me a target.

One day while I was in the motor pool with the platoon, a few soldiers were doing some work and I volunteered to stay over lunch so the soldiers could go to eat. Well, I just happened to be in the same area as this guy and heard him start to address me in a disrespectful manner in front of soldiers. I warned him a few times to keep his comments to himself or he would end up in a situation that he might not be able to get out of if he persisted in messing with me. Well, the words started to become *four-letter*

136

words, and I told him he needed to leave the area. With my Post-Traumatic Stress Disorder (PTSD), we ended up getting into a major altercation and he wanted to press charges on me for assault with a deadly weapon. Let's just say I picked up something in the motor pool that was near me because I had enough of this guy calling me names in front of the soldiers.

By this time I was sitting in the 1SG office wondering if I was going to have a career the next day or not because all these guys were buddies and I was kind of outnumbered. The Platoon Sergeant came in and told me and my 1SG requested a Change of Rating to my Noncommissioned Officers Evaluation Report (NCOER) for disrespect to Senior NCO and assault to Senior NCO. I just about broke down but managed to hold it together. However, I did not sign it because, realizing the situation I was in, I felt as though I had been set up. This was stirring for months, and I knew that the command was trying to get rid of me because the SFC Board was coming up. This was the best way to make sure I would not be on the promotion list in the future.

It did not take long for my NCOER COR to be complete, but it looked really blank to me, so the Lieutenant sat me down and basically read me my rights as a soldier and recommended I receive some kind of punishment for my action on this day. Thank God the Commander liked me and only gave fifteen/fifteen—fifteen days' restriction to the base and fifteen days extra duty with no loss of rank. I sucked up my punishment like a man and did what I was told. I was also referred to mental health or go work at I CORPS headquarters because I was not wanted in the Battalion any more. It was as if they were throwing their problem away and not helping me because they knew my career was over.

I didn't even see the CSM. I was just given an assignment to report to I CORPS, FORSCOM Headquarters 1SG; and when I got there, he told me, "You are going to be a tour guide at the Fort Lewis Military Museum for the rest of the time I was stationed at Fort Lewis or until I came down on orders to leave."

The next day I showed up for PT in headquarters, and it was a freaking joke. I was asked to come out and instruct Physical Training. I was used to hard-core stuff, but after looking around I had to take it easy on the group. I thought to myself, *This is going to be an easy ride until I leave.* I had no idea what I was about to get myself into because working with preservation of military displays, artifacts, and making sure the museum was ready for operation daily was *no joke*! On top of ground maintenance, painting tanks, weapons displays, and trying to remember the history of each display at the museum and Fort Lewis was a huge task. I wondered if a civilian was going to write my evaluation report in the future and if an officer that I don't even know is going to sign it. Along with everything else, we had to make sure we were the perfect *example* of what a soldier was to look like when we conducted VIP tours of the museum. I won't mention everything we did, but I had one hell of a staff and crew. And let me tell you, we never had one bad complaint from anyone traveling or on tour with us. We always demonstrated professionalism and showed the upmost respect to the fallen military.

So why was I here? Was it to learn about military history? Was someone trying to teach me a lesson or take me away from the leadership of being a hard charger? I was always out in front, in combat with soldiers, and never giving up, trying to be the best. Was it time for me to stand aside and watch my peers get selected over me and carry the torch? After all those months, working in that museum, I finally got to meet my rater who was a Full Bird Colonel at the I CORPS Headquarters level. He just happened to be a Field Artillery Officer. I sat down with him, and we had a long talk. I asked him, "Do you think working in the museum is going to hinder my career?" He told me, "We get put in places because the Army has needs for us and sometimes we need a break or time to ourselves. It's not like we are never going to see combat ever again." He was right on that thought!

Are you ready for a shock? My NCOER was submitted to the president of the SFC Board, and when the results came out in August 2000, I was the only person in 1-37 FA BN who made that promotion list. You should have seen the heads rolls and the mad MFers that tried to get my name pulled from the list. All they could deal with was that I was number 62, and I was on my way to Fort Riley, Kansas, to be a Platoon Sergeant. They didn't get this whole ordeal. One thing I know is there are different sides to the military, and I think that every soldier while they serve should learn some kind of military history about their job or the history of their unit. They should want to learn about their patches and the ribbons they wear on their uniforms. PTSD is like a drug, but it will always stay with us.

For me, I had to deal with more demons in my career and in more combat situations. Thank *God* someone was looking over me that day because I learned someone did not know how to write a proper NCOER and it was *incomplete* for the *record* and never made it to my *official* file. I know there is someone who watches over me and tries really hard to help me control my PTSD and the problems I have in life. This could have been *ugly*, but I learned my lesson, and I hope that Platoon Sergeant learned his as well. I hope he picks my book up someday to read this because if he thinks I turned out to be a failure, guess again. For the soldiers, the NCOs, and Officers of the unit I was in, I'm sorry I was the soldier that they made an example of; and if you're still serving today with soldiers or NCOs or even Officers who think they might have a slight problem with PTSD, try to get them some help. You don't have to hear the stories and figure out where you are going to put them in the future or have to box them up and ship them home.

SAM007

PLATOON SERGEANT'S NIGHTMARE BEFORE THE STORM

Talk about getting yourself into a situation! Try being a Platoon Sergeant for Charlie battery 4-1 FA, and they tell you to start preparing your guys for deployment to Kuwait/Iraq because Operation Iraqi Freedom is soon to kick off sometime in the future. We have already been to the National Training Center and to the field several times, but I am still planning on my training events for the future before we ship out.

Now I want you know that I'm now Sergeant First Class and I eat, sleep, and drink Army. My family is my Platoon, but I know my guys don't like me because they are not used to a guy like me who is hard on them. It is important to me to ensure they know right from wrong. I have been hearing there are new Platoon Sergeants coming to the Battery, but whose place was he taking and who was getting promoted? I knew for sure the 1SG didn't like me and was looking for every chance to find a way to get rid of me. However, I was determined to take my soldiers to combat because it is every Platoon Sergeant's dream to take his Platoon into combat. The thing that helped me was that I was a single guy and devoted to my job. They knew I wanted this job and that I wanted to lead my soldiers into combat.

There were times when my soldiers got on my nerves, really got under my skin, and I had to walk away. I was hiding that I had Post-Traumatic Stress Disorder (PTSD), and I damn sure did not want anyone to know what happened in my last unit. I was not sure if the leadership was trying to dig some stuff up on me or not, but it soon started to surface. We began getting word that things were getting bad in the Middle East. After 911 my whole Platoon sat in the dayroom and watched the twin towers fall, and we knew this was not a good sign. When are we going? Leadership had no answers for them while their country was under fire and people were dying. At the last minute, things had to be packed. It was nighttime, and the soldiers were tired. I could see it in their eyes and faces. We haven't even hit Kuwait yet, and the soldiers looked broken, but this must go on. We had our share of soldiers who tried to get out of deployments, but somehow they still ended up going with us. Unfortunately, these soldiers ended up being a much larger problem in Kuwait before we got to Iraq.

The process to get to Kuwait was stressful, and it was their first time away from home for some of the guys. They had no way to reach out to talk to anyone, so battle buddies was our number-one thing. I think the guys thought I was trying to be hard on them, but when I got to the Platoon, only three of us were wearing combat patches. Those without combat patches wanted to do their own thing. I'll tell you, when we arrived in Kuwait and stepped off the aircraft, it was really hot. Some of the soldiers could not take the heat. It was nighttime when we arrived in theater. It was windy and hot, and sand was blowing all over the place. Some guys were in Alpha Battery when we deployed to Operation Desert Spring last year, and it was not like this. Where were we going? They loaded us on buses, told us not to look out the windows, and to stay quiet. I think we were on the buses for about three to four hours, and then we got to our Forward Operation Base (FOB) in Kuwait, in middle of the desert, in the middle of nowhere.

I could tell the guys were stressed, and there was tension between the guys in the platoon. We hadn't had a good meal in days, and things just seemed to go downhill. Every day we were outside the tents training in the hot, sandy desert with our protective gear in case we were gassed in Iraq. This training started to get old, and we started to repeat a lot of stuff over and over. But it had to be done. I think my stress level was building as well because some of soldiers were starting to disrespect me and started to talk back. They had gotten too comfortable with me and thought they could because I was their friend. I don't think so! I really won't explain the type of situation I got into with one of my soldiers, but it landed me in front of my 1SG. When the incident happened, members of the battalion staff were standing right there and this situation was brought up to the Command

141

Sergeant Major (CSM). At first, I was not living in leadership tent with the other Platoon Sergeants, but I was sleeping at the end of the tent with my platoon. My CSM asked me, "How I liked sleeping with the lower enlisted soldiers and if I wanted the information of what I did to another soldier to be leaked?" So for my action in preparation in combat, I was removed from my Platoon Sergeant's position and replaced with this "No time in grade" Platoon Sergeant I spoke about in the beginning of my story. I was told to report to Headquarters battery and not to talk to any soldiers in my Platoon until I was instructed to do so. Lots of the soldiers had questions about what happened because they had lost their leader for combat. I guess the new guy was already groomed to fit in, and that was the plan all along. It was about three days before the CSM sat with me and explained to me exactly what my mission would be once I met my mentor. When he explained my job to me, I knew my career was finally over if I made out of Iraq alive.

When he told me that I would be the Battalion Reenlist NCO or Advisor to the Commander, I called it. I was not school trained in this crappie job, and back at Fort Riley we all laughed at this guy because he just sat around and did nothing. The next day I sat down with this older guy, and we talked about each other's careers. We talked about him retiring and his plan for when he got to Iraq or if he was even going to Iraq because if I was on board he was on a flight out of here and working reenlistments from home. I asked him if this was the plan the whole time, to bring him to Kuwait and have me become the Advisor Counselor for soldiers' careers. He said, "Yes, your name came up, and CSM wanted you to be in this position in Iraq and didn't think you should have a platoon in combat." This NCO gave me a special protective suitcase with a computer and printout of soldiers' names with the options of what they could get, including some flags and battalion pins. He told me my call sign on the radio and walked away. I don't think I ever saw him again. That day I knew I had one hell of a mission because this was not an easy job back home and it is damn sure not going to be easy in combat.

We made our road march up to Iraq during night hours, and it was super windy and hard to see the enemy. You never knew who the enemy was or if the enemy was watching as we moved forward. As soon as I hit the ground in Baghdad, Iraq, I was looking for soldiers on my list. At first, they were only a number to me because I was trying to make numbers. When the CSM counseled me, he said, "We have to make numbers." I had no training on what to say or to even present to the soldiers when I found them. So I sat down and looked at some options because if I was going to make this a successful mission, I needed a plan. CSM was not helping me, and I did not have an office or really anywhere to bring the soldiers for a discussion about what I could offer them or the needs of the Army. I took my plan to CSM, and he thought it was a joke. He asked, "Where I was going to get the money in combat to build an office or set something up for the soldiers?" I told him, "Let me control this, and I'll make happen." I did! I got with Iraqi contractors who were setting up an Internet cafe in the FOB to let me use a building with space that was bombed out. I cleaned it out and got the Internet installed in my small office. I found a couch and desk, and I was open for business. I wanted to make my office a comfortable place so we could forget we were in combat zone. With training from Career Counselors, daily trips of putting my life on the line day after day, going on supply runs to get my options and numbers for retention, and showing up to command and staff meetings at higher headquarters each night, I made the mission for the second, third, and fourth quarters. I started using MWR funds to orders T-shirts and hats with our BN logo on it when soldiers reenlisted. They would get a hat or a T-shirt when they reenlisted in theater. I was getting so good at this that I was able to get the options the soldier was requesting. Some of the soldiers were walking out of Iraq with $20,000-tax free reenlistment bonuses. Our favorite spot to reenlist soldiers was the *Cross Sabers* in Iraq. I started getting tons of soldiers, but it was at a cost. I went on raids, check-points, patrols, and sat at check-points and supply runs, putting my life on line to talk to soldiers to find out what they wanted for reenlistment options.

I even took part on nightly raids with the Headquarters' battery as Truck/Commander because the guys were short of manpower. I did my job while assigned to the command, but that whole time the BN CSM and the BDE CSM did not like me for what I did back in Kuwait to that soldier. They held a grudge against me when it was time to write awards. I was asked by the headquarters' battery commander to sit down with him because he was the approving authority to endorse my Bronze Star write up that was sent up for signature for the BDE commander. That day, while I standing in the awards formation, I saw the awards clerk with all the Bronze Stars laid out ready to be presented. I was up there with my brothers in arms and some of them didn't do a thing, but we were all up there for a purpose. I noticed something as the commander got closer and closer to me. The awards disappeared, and there were none when they got to me.

Then BDE Commander called me out in front of the whole Battalion and read this: "Supervised Total Army Retention Program for a five-hundred-member Field Artillery Battalion while engaged in systemic warfare operation and exceeded retention goal by 159 percent of personnel that were planning on departing the service while deployed to Operation Iraqi Freedom I and II."

He presented me the third BDE *Bulldog belt buckle* for all my hard work in Iraq. I thought to myself, *What really was my purpose? Was this a punishment for someone to be laughed at by the whole battalion and to not even get an award for going above and beyond? Were they saying that too many Bronze Stars were submitted from our battalion and that my award was not justified?*

I served as a special staff advisor to the Director (Commander) and the Department Manager (Command Sergeant Major) while attending to matters relating to retention, career development, separations, and attrition management.

I provided expert guidance and assistance to the Battalion Commander regarding training and career (Recruitment/Classification) program matters and assisted Soldiers in developing career goals and plans on how to achieve set goals.

"Sergeant First Class Stephens' phenomenal ability to react to situational awareness and reaction to combat situation, immediately and enthusiastically assumed responsibility for a challenging and unique mission on the morning of August 8, 2003, when his counterparts where attacked by RPG and roadside bomb (IED). Him and the other members of the Headquarters drivers and members of the senior Leadership risk their lives, as they made themselves an obstacle to obscure the enemy just enough of time to get a MEDAVAC on the ground and to get soldiers from Eighty-Second EOD and Service Battery 4-1 FA Ammo Section out of the area before it was secured from the enemy."

I provided expert guidance and assistance to a sixty-man Platoon and their families regarding training and career program matters, ability to identify management barriers and/or problems that adversely affect career growth Recruitment/Classification opportunities in order to implement strategies that remedy obstacles.

I oversaw all phases of planning during wartime operations, implementing and administering the platoon-wide training program.

I supervised six Staff Line Supervisors who worked under my direct leadership and developed an expert mentorship program to help educate fifteen section leaders and sixty team members about military leadership and civilian education.

I maintained oversight of computer equipment. I maintained accurate inventory controls and possessed a courier card required to hand carried secure equipment and documents.

I evaluated the career and training programs to determine Soldiers' effectiveness.

My award recommendation read to the commander:

The mission goes on to the next assignment, as the Post-Traumatic Stress Disorder grows inside, held in like a shell hiding and waiting to come out but when.

Thank you for nothing!

SAM007

A TRANSITION IN AND OUT OF THE HOSPITAL AND WAR AND RECOVERY

On October 31, 2008, for twenty years and twenty-one days I severed. I said my farewell to my family, my career, and my love. It was the life I longed for and would never look back on because I was a broken warrior that could not serve my country anymore. After numerous combat missions and peace-keeping deployments to the Middle East, my final tour was to start a new chapter in life as a retired veteran and soon to become civilian. I stood on the parade field at Fort Meade, Maryland, as the Old Guard retired a few of us. My little girl watched the ceremony in which she can remember today as her father and her superhero say good-bye to the United States Army.

I look back today and try to remember my steps from being nineteen years old when I left for Desert Shield/Desert Storm to my final days in Iraq helping the Army, write for the Center of Army Lessons Learned (CALL), and to my last ribbon placed on my uniform for my retirement ceremony. I will never know what my future could have been if I had accepted that fifth combat tour. Where would I be today? Would I be that Command Sergeant Major I always dreamed of being with my peers today? Or would I have died because of getting into a situation I could not have handled due to the Post-Traumatic Stress Disorder (PTSD) getting so bad.

I believe that I took the right road because I'm here today writing my story and I have a little girl I can share my experiences with so she can pass it down through her next generations. Even though there are some who want to forget the nightmares, every day I experience reminders of being in a combat situation or flashbacks of those days. The best thing to do is talk to someone or to write about it.

That brings me to the Warrior Transition Unit at Walter Reed Army Medical Center in Washington, D. C. Something was just not right when I returned back from Iraq on my last deployment. I wasn't really there for combat, and I didn't feel safe either because we didn't have much protection while we were there. The leadership was more interested in getting the data or the book finished and out of the Area of Operation than having concern for our *safety*, I guess. I felt rushed in the current situation. Over all, it did turn out to be a successful operation and we got credit for the book. Some officers got more credit than others in their career, and it seemed they got more credit than we did. But I guess that's politics in the military.

I guess it was a few months that I had been back from Iraq and I was waiting for the Master Sergeant Board results to come out. My Sergeant Major called me into his office and sat me down to tell me that he didn't think I was ever going to make it to MSG because this rating period I was going to get a two block on my Evaluation Report from him. I looked at him in shock because I had just redeployed from Iraq and he didn't even send a note or visit the five of us while we were there. As a special team, I thought for sure this was my punch ticket. I guess there are always career killers in your field. I couldn't say anything but decided to take leave for a while. While I was on leave, I came down on assignment for my fifth combat tour to deployment to Afghanistan. Knowing what my Sergeant Major told me, I had a long talk with my wife. I told her that I knew we were having problems and the PTSD was getting worse. I found that there were programs to help soldiers with PTSD, so I went to the doctors and they evaluated me. I was told to go see a doctor at Walter Reed Army Medical Center. In late 2006 I was diagnosed with severe Post-Traumatic Stress Disorder, and they recommended treatment at WTU. I reported back to my unit with orders assigned to WTU in Washington, D. C. My SGM was so mad that he told me I would never make it anywhere in my career again and he would see to it. I knew my career was over because once I gave the okay for treatment, all my rights as a soldier were gone. I was like a guinea pig, and I was under control of the WTU. I had to move into the barracks and stay there for one year for treatment or until I was ready to come home to my family.

At first it was as if there was nothing wrong with you as all your body parts are intact. You're walking around seeing soldiers who come off the battlefield all blown up with missing limbs or blind or just not quite normal. But for me, I have PTSD which is hidden and people just look at me like I'm SFC/E7 with some problems. It is a lot different when you get to the Psychiatric Department and you meet the group you're going to be with for the next year. No one has a rank or a last name. They just have a first name, and everyone is in their own little shell, kind of like shell shock at first. No one talks to anyone unless you're infantry. The infantry guys have some special bond, and they just click with each other. They like to talk about killing shit and people in Iraq. At first we did a lot of sitting and waiting for the doctors to call us, talk to us, and ask us how our day was. There were times when we thought about killing ourselves or felt suicidal. It was the same stuff every day. But then we started therapy as a group, and this is how we bonded. Some days, people in our group talked about things that were on their minds or something they saw while they were there. Sometimes, it took them a whole year to come out of their shell. I won't disclose a lot of information because most of this I want to keep private out of respect for the group I served with in the WTU. I guess you could say they took me back in combat with their stories and pictures they drew and shared with us. I wish I could say I kept in touch with them, but I haven't. We all went our separate ways because we wanted it that way. Someday I hope some or one of them will pick up my book and read it because you or the group will always be on my mind. If it was just cutting out pictures from magazines or listening to music to describe how you felt about yourself or light therapy or just talking to one another in the waiting room.

While I was there I learned that Post-Traumatic Stress Disorder was not just a battlefield disease. PTSD comes in different forms as I learned from the many stories in my group. That's one reason why I am trying to send the message out to everyone to let them know PTSD is a real thing and a slow killer. It is a hidden killer. It's sad that a lot of us have it and will not speak up about it. We are too proud of ourselves, think we are better than others, the VA is too far, or we just don't want the support. Kids, soldiers, NCOs, officers, family members, grandparents, and combat veterans—all could have this. We never know who could have this hidden killer living inside us.

I don't know where I would be today without treatment. I do know that when I was at the WTU it was difficult to talk to people because when the injury is not noticeable, people don't look at you like a fallen warrior. I noticed the guys and gals in wheelchairs got a lot of special treatment, and I saw this doing job fairs and special events. We were outsiders, and because we have PTSD, we are left out of the crowd. I experienced this while I was in the WTU when I went to the gym. People looked at me like, "Why are you here in this gym, and what's wrong with you?" When you talk to someone, they have a better understanding where you're coming from and what your purpose is in life. If we don't tell our story, the people are not going to understand our treatment and the VA is not going to help us. I have to admit that the best assignment I ever had was where people take care of people at the WTU. The soldiers, NCOs, and officers who volunteered for the assignments or worked at the WTU put their heart and soul into helping our wounded warriors put their lives back together and get on track. For some it was just a stepping stone, but others I could tell they did every day in their lives and they were there for a purpose. I didn't always agree with all the programs they had, but I have to agree with the command and control they had because it helped me to do so much more after therapy. The nice thing about WTU was all the big job companies were right there. I mean major companies like the Department of Defense, etc. were there to support the wounded warrior if needed. A lot of these soldiers got their break here after the service. At night I could not go home to my family, so I worked on my resume. My resume skills were not the best, so I looked at other resumes online or my buddies' resumes I served with, and they helped me because they knew my career was over.

The situation I found myself in made me fight for my security status. I didn't do anything wrong and saw no reason to lose my security status because I served my country well. I just had Post-Traumatic Stress Disorder!

I fought and won because that's the only thing I had left to help get where I am today in life. I tell you, I did not sit on my butt. I started to get to the job fairs and met a few people. I started *networking* and found that *networking* was the key to my success in life. I met a few gentlemen from a Department of Defense Agency, and they asked me to do an internship with them while I was assigned to active duty and the WTU. Let me tell you, these guys took me under their wings and trained me to know what I know today, and I will never forget the mentors in my life. I wish them the very best in their successful careers. PTSD can be a doormat in your life. For me, I've worked in an office environment and have been going to counseling every month. I have been talking to people about my problems to help cope with my demons. I don't have bullets flying at me or people removing me from my combat positions. I don't think my PTSD had gotten any better when I got home to my family because I just could not get along with my wife. PTSD has taken me away from my family, and I live alone dealing with my demons myself at night.

It's good that I have a nice place to come home to at night to relax. I don't have to worry about extra work, college work, or all kinds of bills and paperwork piling up. I sometimes write to express my feelings, but most of time I'm watching TV or I am on social media seeing what's new. It's great that I can wake up, go over and have breakfast with my father every day in the morning, and relax. I drive to work, do my job, and protect the people that have to be protected in case something happens in the real world. People believe in me and know that I will take care of the situation before it becomes a problem. While they are working, they never have to worry because I have it under control. The world has many different problems, but PTSD is just one of them. I'm happy I have the friends that I can sit down with and talk to about my problems. If you have a problem, I hope what you read beyond these pages will help you cope with your demons. As I stood on that parade field for the last time on Halloween, I wondered, *What is my next step, and where is this all going to take me?* At least, I can look back and say it's been one *hell* of ride! I won't miss any of it, and I never go back again because my life was spared for some reason.

SAM007

WAR OF GOD

God is the reason we have war and have had biblical wars for years. The other day while I lay in the hospital, a chaplain came in to see me and ask me, "If I needed anything special from the word of *God*." I just lay there and said, "Who is *God*?" Because there are many gods that we all pray to, and if it wasn't for *God*, I would not be lying here today. This world will always be at some kind of war between one another because people will always die. I think by this time I caught her attention because the air was silent. I asked her, "How would it feel to live in a total world of peace?" She would not have a job, and those who create weapons for war would not have jobs because we would not be at war with each other.

I understand that people say we fight for *God* and country, but we really don't, because look what our people have done to *God* in this country. They removed him from our money and our schools and even banned him from public events. Do you still say you fight for *God* to protect our country? Our country was built on the founding fathers and the right of *freedom*. That is why we live in the country. We are not here to die for *God*. We die for our *freedom* and for our people to be free. Other countries die for their gods because when terrorists attack us they use their god's name when going to death or attacking us. You don't hear American's screaming, "*God, God, God*" when they are attacking the enemy in other countries in combat.

Listening to a former friend who was an Infantry Chaplain who buried 150 of his soldiers, lost his own driver, and picked up a weapon in combat to survive on the battlefield, I can see why he gave up his cross and *God* for the life he lives today. War, why do we have it? Why do we have to lose the many men and women when they go to battle? Are we really winning that war?

Many different visions of our Lord and God, but overall from my view in life, we all serve the same purpose here for one *God*. A *God* is a *God*, and we will fight until the end, until life remains no more and we are all gone. *God* will be as one. The world will be no more.

Getting back to the hospital room, I told the lady chaplain that I believe in *God*, though it might not be the *God* that she believes in. If I did not have a faith, I would not have made it through my combat tours or multiple deployments to tell my story. I told her there are more people out there hurting than me and she should be in other rooms spreading the word of faith to someone who her creator is about to take.

She was speechless as she looked at me and said, "Thank you for your story." I think that day I changed her life on the way she looks at *God* and why we fight for our country's wars and our freedom. I am not the word of *God*, and I am not here to spread rumors, but every author has their view on life. My past was tough on me with several breakups and a divorce, separation of a child, and a terrible disorder I have to live with the rest of my life—Post-Traumatic Stress Disorder. All I'm asking is for you to make the right choice when you make decisions in life because sometimes you can't go back. It may be too late to rebuild the wall you have torn down. One *God* and only one *God* lives among us, and no one will ever understand until we destroy each other and with weapons of mass destruction (WMD) or *God* himself.

SAM007

THE CLOSING OF THE MIRROR

Thank you to the people who hurt me in this life because you have motivated me to do what I've always wanted to do to. I never want to hurt you. All I want is for you to see what you were getting yourself into with having nothing, no bond whatever. There is a special someone, but who are you? If you read this, you will know who you are. Never to forget what we had. This book is for you because I've done my damage. Everyone will know what we have both been through. Now my mind is clear. I can sit back, relax, and start a new chapter in life. I put this story on these pages so all could see the darkness that we were hiding from the world.

Go into a room with a mirror, look into it, and tell me what you see? Now if you can, take the mirror off the wall and be careful not to break it, or seven years bad luck could follow you place to place. You are holding the mirror as it appears to have two sides. Look at the dark side because this represents my side. This is past that you put me through. Not everyone has a shiny side, not even you.

Now you know the truth! Thank you for taking the time to buy this book and read it. It has taken me more than enough time to gather my thoughts. The truth is out, and I put my mind to it. Those who hold a copy of this book, think back to what you told me before I started writing it. Now I bet you feel really bad? I guess now you would consider being my friend or close companion. *Think again!*

Before we go, don't forget to put the mirror back on the wall. If you don't put the mirror back on the wall, I'll pull you through the next one you look through. I can move throughout the many mirrors in this world looking for you. It would suck not to be able to look in a mirror ever again because I would be waiting to make you one of my mirror people.

SAM007

COVER TO COVER

A lot of people ask me why I did not use this title for my book, think about it! A lot of people read daily, but many of us just skim through the pages of a book. Like me, some of us have never read an entire book in our life. So my story starts here. I guess I can go back to high school when I was in lower-level classes and I just picked areas out of the book to read for homework and never really read the whole book but just discussed it in class.

I can't recall in my entire life if I ever read a complete book from cover to cover. So pointing this out, I was never much of a reader, didn't follow directions, and rarely paid attention in school. I wasn't an honor grad student or the typical A's and B's student either, but I got by, and I was more into arts and drafting, you might say. However, I enjoyed American history, and for some reason I was fascinated with history in general. I did pretty well in that subject. I was not someone who read a book in my spare time for enjoyment. When I was in middle school, I can't remember reading any books all the way through. I just hit the main parts and got by in this manner.

High school was a struggle for me because I wasn't a very smart kid. First, my upbringing was not the best because my parents never finished school and they worked in a carpet factory most of their lives. My father smoked and drank all his paycheck up with no regard for his family. It didn't sit well with me, and a lot my friends made fun of my parents and the weight problems of my sister and my mother. Because my father was a drunk, my friends made fun of him as well. I was always uncomfortable when my friends came over because my dad was always chasing my friends out of the house or yelling at my mother. On top of all of this, we were a middle class family barely getting by without a car. My parents both had *epilepsy*. My mother was much worse than my father, and he always told me "I got it from the Army and combat."

Boy, I had to live with the "*no car*" jokes forever, plus all the rumors that my friends spread about me in grade school which carried all the way through high school. How would you like to go through school and not have a girlfriend ever? Well, there were a few brave ones I must say and thank you for that. I wasn't much of a jock or a smart guy in high school. I was more of an outcast. We all had our groups back in the day, and I was a skate rat because I didn't have a car. My mode of transportation was my skateboard, and I made some cool friends who today I can say I am still professional friends with, and they also have professional careers and families.

One of my favorite pictures has me sitting on the shoulder of evil emperor ex-president Saddam Hussein that was a part of the four heads palace at the Al-Man-Sur district in Bagdad, Iraq. Our unit, Fourth Battalion, First Field Artillery, part of Task Force Gunner for the First Armored Division and the POTUS, was selected to remove these large concrete heads from each corner of the palace once Saddam Hussein's power was overthrown. This was to show the Iraq people he was no longer in political power. I like this picture because I was a part of this history-making ordeal in this country before the heads where melted down for separate commodities. The stories of people and families I talked to with the same thing I'm dealing with on a daily basis to include a collection of poems I have written over my lifetime are included in this book. These findings helped me during my writer's block and with my mental relaxation during my healing process with my Post-Traumatic Stress Disorder (PTSD) at Walter Reed Army Medical Center between 2007 and 2008.

I'm hoping the story of my life, with my combat experiences and my experiences with PTSD with my own family and friends, reaches out to all the veterans. I also included how I am dealing with my corporate life as well. I'm not looking for the fame and glory or money behind this, as most of it will be used making books and selling them to the great people who read books about people's lives. In the end, I just want people to read my book from cover to cover and spread the word because there truly is a story to be told here and for the truth to be known.

William A. Stephens Jr.
US Army (Ret.)

SAM007

ABOUT THE AUTHOR

Sergeant First Class William A. Stephens Jr. (Ret.) was born in Carlisle, Pennsylvania, in 1969. Upon graduating from Carlisle Senior High School, Mr. Stephens enlisted in the United States Army in October 1988. Throughout his twenty years of distinguished military service, he has held positions of leadership ranging in experience from Senior Enlisted Advisor, Battalion Career Counselor, Platoon Sergeant, Gunnery Sergeant, Howitzer Section Chief, Cannon Crewmember, Battalion Intelligence Sergeant, Senior Observer Controller Trainer, and Battalion Security Manager. Upon retirement from the military with distinction, Mr. Stephens continued leadership roles in the civilian workforce through completion of the internship with the Defense Security Service, employed as a Pennsylvania State Corrections Officer, and Department of the Defense employee.

Mr. Stephens' assignments include Mechanicsburg, Camp Hill, New Cumberland, Pennsylvania; Fort Dix, New Jersey; Fort Sill, Oklahoma; Fort Lewis, Washington; Fort Carson, Colorado; Fort Riley, Kansas; and Walter Reed Army Medical Center, Washington, D. C., as a part of the Wounded Warrior Transition Brigade. Mr. Stephens deployed multiple times to overseas locations including four combat deployments to Kuwait/Saudi Arabia as a part of Operation Desert Shield and Operation Desert Storm. In 2006 he completed his fourth tour to Iraq/Southwest Asia as a part of Operation Iraqi Freedom/Liberation of Iraq, the Transition of Iraq, and National Resolution of Iraq where his assignment was instrumental in collecting battlefield strategy data. As a result of his research efforts and compilation of "war" data, Mr. Stephens developed the Security Forces Handbook as a significant contributing author for the *Center of Army*

Lessons Learned. This handbook was mandated for soldiers deploying to battlefield locations to provide better insight and "real examples" for soldiers as well as to limit casualties in the war zones.

He is a graduate of the Army's First Sergeant Course where he was selected as the First Sergeant of his class and has completed all levels of leadership courses throughout the Army. He is a graduate of the Army Antiterrorism Level I and Level II Course, Security Managers Course, and Total Army Instructor Trainers Course. Just before graduation from college with a degree in Leadership, he turned his focus toward Personnel Security. Upon retirement, Mr. Stephens graduated as the Student Leader of his class in 2009 from the Class 667C Pennsylvania Department of Corrections Training Academy. He is working on a Physical Security Course and part of the Department of Defense Security Professional Education Development Program. He plans to take the Physical Security Fundamentals Certification Course by the end of 2018 and 2019.

Military awards received include the Joint Service Commendation Medal, (3) Meritorious Service Medals, (10) Army Commendation Medals, (10) Army Achievement Medals, Military Outstanding Volunteer Service Medal, Southwest Asia Service Medal with (3) Bronze Campaign Stars, and the Iraq Campaign Medal with (3) Bronze Service Stars, (2) Valorous Unit Award, (2) Army Superior Unit Award, (6) Army Good Conduct Medal, (2) National Defense Service Medal, Bronze Service Star, Armed Forces Expeditionary Medal, Army Service Ribbon, (4) Overseas Service Ribbon, and Korean Defense Service Medal. Mr. Stephens was recognized for his efforts by receipt of the Major General "Aubrey Red Newman" award for outstanding Counseling and Mentorship and as well as a member of the Sergeant Audie Murphy Club for outstanding Military Leadership. He is an active member of the Wounded Warrior Project and provides presentations to other veterans on behalf of the project. In 2011–12, Mr. Stephens was recognized for his hard work by the CFC and received the Central Pennsylvania Golden Star Leaders Award. In his spare time, Mr. Stephens has started public speaking for the cause of PTSD and other local organizations, volunteers as a CFC Campaign coordinator, and assists with the Pennsylvania Adult Special Olympics and the installation of the children's Christmas program for disadvantaged youth.

It takes the courage and strength of a warrior to ask for help.

Special dedication to my father William Alfred Stephens Sr. from October 25, 1933 to September 4, 2017 (Rest in Peace). He will always be looking down on his grandchildren as a warrior of his own and father of his own. I wish you would have been around to see the success of your son and to carry the Stephens name with honor and pride. I will make you happy and proud and be the voice of the voiceless to all. Your death came so sudden, and now you're with Mom. Enjoy your eternal walk in heaven forever.

We will miss you, Pappy Bill, on special days like my daughter's birthday, Thanksgiving, at Christmastime, and on your birthday.

Time to say good-bye and close the many pages of the book.

SAM007

CPSIA information can be obtained
at www.ICGtesting.com
Printed in the USA
BVHW030824110119
537557BV00003B/11/P